getting lucky

getting

matt cohen

lucky

stories

Alfred A. Knopf Canada

PUBLISHED BY ALFRED A. KNOPF CANADA

Copyright © 2000 by Matt Cohen

All rights reserved under International and Pan-American Copyright
Conventions. Published in 2000 by Alfred A. Knopf Canada, a division
of Random House of Canada Limited, Toronto. Distributed by
Random House of Canada Limited, Toronto.

Knopf Canada and colophon are trademarks.

Slightly different versions of some of the stories in this collection were originally
published as follows: "Edward/Eduardo" in *Story* magazine, Summer 1999;
"Winter" in *Toronto Life*, Summer 1997; "Literary Synapses" in *Brick*, Spring 1998;
"Napoleon in Moscow" *Descant*, Spring 1998; and "Shelter" in *Toronto Life*, Summer 1999.

Canadian Cataloguing in Publication Data

Cohen, Matt, 1942–1999
 Getting lucky

ISBN 0-676-97246-2

I. Title

PS 8555.O4G47 2000
PR9199.3.C63G47 2000   C813'.54   C99-932755-0

First Edition

Printed and bound in the United States of America

10 9 8 7 6 5 4 3 2 1

For Patsy and the children:
Coca, Seth, Daniel and Madeleine

contents

getting
lucky

"**M**ichael," the woman said. "That's quite a name." She leaned across the table and squinted at his face as though it were a book with small print. "Michael. Now there's a name that says something to me." She leaned back. "It says quiet, thoughtful, someone who's got a lot more inside himself than he likes to show. Someone you could trust to hold your purse." She smiled at Michael. Her eye teeth were just a little bit too long and it gave her a look that Michael thought might explain why she wasn't here with a man. Then he was ashamed of himself for judging a woman by her teeth and reminded himself that he had chosen to sit opposite her because she had looked both attractive and available. "But not your credit cards," she said and smiled again, this time tilting her head, and in this new light, her eye teeth didn't look so bad.

"Do you have a lot more inside than you show?"

Michael looked down at his hands. He knew he was someone who kept to himself, but he couldn't have offered a list of what he was keeping. There were, he supposed, all those feelings and thoughts for which he didn't have words, and then there were the ones for which he did have words but also had the sense not to say.

Would this woman, for example, really want to know that he thought her eye teeth were a social handicap? That he was wondering if she was some kind of vampire? That the way her eyes sparked reminded him of his father's dogs when they caught the scent of something they knew they could kill? That he wished he could untie his tongue, look into her face, tell her stories about herself that would put her in his power the way she had suddenly taken control of him, trapped and wrapped him in her charm so completely that he was just like a boy on a toboggan, speeding down an icy hill wanting to go faster and faster until he crashed.

Karen opened the door and motioned Michael to go in first. He moved towards the only light, which was a television set showing a hockey game, no sound. It was that playoff time of year. In front of the television set, sitting in a big stuffed chair, was a bald man with a long storky neck. As Michael came closer he saw the man was slowly swaying back and forth, eyes closed, as though either praying or in a trance. Maybe it was the reflection of the ice, but the man's skin seemed absolutely white, almost transparent, in fact he was so absolutely hairless that even his eyelids were totally bald and ended in twin pink curves that matched his lips. He had a long curved blade of a nose that was like some kind of aerodynamic ornament.

"That's Bob," Karen said.

"I'm Karen," Karen had said after the bit about his name at the tavern. She was wearing a white short-sleeved shirt and slacks, no ring, and Michael had thought she might work at a hospital or a drugstore. She'd separated him off from the group without him resisting, then said he could drive her home.

"You can come in for a coffee and then we'll see," she said when they got to her place, a shabby Insulbrick bungalow in the north end of Kingston. But she hadn't mentioned anything about this Bob.

Karen waved him down the hall and Michael followed her to the kitchen. She motioned him to sit down at the table. Half of it was piled with books like *Know Your Aura* and *Secrets of Tibetan Meditation*. Coffee cups, toast crumbs and two identical jars of strawberry jam provided the rest of the decoration.

"Bob your roommate?" Michael asked.

"Kind of. We never got married but once it was like we were."

Michael looked down at his hands. For luck he had worn a cowboy shirt to the tavern; his sister Sadie had given it to him last year for his thirty-third birthday, along with a card saying "Jesus Was a Cowboy," and it had real pearl buttons. In the bright light of the kitchen it looked as stupid as he'd feared it would.

"That's something," Michael said. "That you could change from one to the other and still stay friends."

Karen had slightly waved hair, so black it might have been dyed, strong puffed features. Not bad-looking, could be anywhere in her thirties. When she'd cleaned the table and put the kettle on she sat opposite him. There was something he'd been on the edge of noticing all evening, the way she looked at him: direct, like a man. He imagined himself calling his sister the next day to say he'd worn her shirt for luck and he'd ended up with a woman who looked like a man and a man who looked like a freak.

"Tell me what you're thinking," Karen said.

"About the man in the living room."

"Bob?"

"Yeah."

"He had brain cancer. That's what happened to his hair. Now he takes morphine pills. Says he has put human life behind him and is going to spend the rest of his time on earth bathing in his cosmic aura."

"That's something," Michael said. Before they split up he and Lee-Anne had tried going to a group she'd found at the Cosmic Therapy Centre. One night the leader had told them to take off all their clothes and lie with their heads together, their feet sticking out like spokes of a wagon wheel. They all had to hold hands and pretend they were joined to the One Being. At first Michael had felt horny, even though everyone but Lee-Anne looked pretty ugly, and he'd wondered if they would be instructed to have group sex. Finally he managed to concentrate and what came into his head was a picture of an ice cream cone.

"I suppose you think that kind of thing is stupid," Karen said. She had lit a cigarette and blew the smoke out, almost right at Michael, as though daring him to say something bad about Bob.

He wanted to reach out and smooth that dark wave of too-black hair away from her eyes.

He wanted to let her know that he could see—in her swollen features, her quick way of moving her hands, the way her mouth twisted around her words—how angry she was.

He wanted to be tender with her, the way you would be tender with an animal that had been badly treated and just needed some time and space to settle down.

"No," Michael said, "if I had the chance I would probably admire a man like Bob."

They lay down on her bed but without taking off their clothes, except for their shoes. His shirt was part polyester and chafed at the sunburn across his neck.

Michael was on his back and he was thinking this was as far as he wanted to go. Since Lee-Anne had left he'd gotten lucky a couple of times, never at the tavern but at parties, but in the end he hadn't felt so lucky after all.

One woman whose name he'd never known grabbed his head and put it to her breast and it was like he had a tough purple fig in his mouth. She had both her hands on the back of his head and he hadn't been able to break away until the whole thing was over and then he'd tried to act as though it was nothing because he didn't want to hurt her feelings. Not that he was such a great catch himself. Getting into the bath the other day he'd seen his belly in the mirror. It had looked to be such a mistake that he'd punched it, to knock the air out and get it back to its normal shape.

If people loved each other they wouldn't care about their purple figs or their big bellies, but it was hard to love someone you'd hardly even met. Then he thought: it could be hard to be hard for someone you'd hardly even met.

"You okay?" Karen asked. Her voice wasn't hard. It was soft and quiet.

"I'm okay," Michael said. "Almost fell asleep."

"Drink too much?"

"Guess so."

Karen was quiet for a moment and Michael wished his

Jesus Was a Cowboy shirt would float away so Karen's big hospital or druggist hands could rub him down until he was smooth as silk and asleep.

Instead one of Karen's hands had laid itself along his cheek. It traced a path down to his neck; then she shifted and began to unsnap the pearl buttons of his shirt.

"I've got a big stomach," Michael warned.

"I've got big knees," Karen said.

Michael couldn't help snorting. The taste of beer came through his nose and he got a sudden picture of Karen, naked, no details except her knees, which looked like pink hubcaps.

"I'm serious," Karen said. She raised her knee to his chest and brought one of his hands to touch it.

It wasn't the size of a hubcap, or even a soccer ball, but it was impressively round and substantial. Lee-Anne's knees had been like broken bones.

"So?"

"I guess it's pretty big," Michael admitted. "No bigger than mine."

Karen rolled off him and sat up. She started to undo her belt.

"Take off your pants and we'll measure. If your knees are bigger than mine I'll owe you a beer."

Michael folded Karen's hands around his face. He kissed her palms. He liked the palms of her hands. They were full. They had a sweet sour taste with a hint of olive. They would be strong without being rough. He slid them underneath his shirt and when he had them on his sides and they felt the way he hoped they would, he knelt beside her and began taking down her pants. He kissed her impressive knees, which tasted of salt. He ran his hands down the bristle of her shins and up again. Karen was massaging his chest and stomach. He moved between her legs.

"Take your pants off," Karen said. "I want to see your knees. I still think I'm going to win that beer."

In the middle of the night Michael began to dream that a team of men were scraping the paint off the outside of the house. As he floated to consciousness the sound changed to the scraping of chair legs along a hall. When he opened his eyes he saw that the door to Karen's room had opened. Bob was sitting in the hall, a guitar crooked in his arms. Michael reached over to Karen's side of the bed. She was still there. He could hardly hear the sound of her breathing. Bob strummed the guitar and began to play.

You won't miss me when I'm gone
'Cause you've already moved on
To some place I'll never know
Where love is just a weed that grows

Karen shifted in the bed beside Michael. She put her hands behind her head and in the light from the hall Michael could see the shadows settling into the hollows of her arms.

"Nicely put, Bob," Karen said.

"Thanks."

"I like that part about love being a weed. If love is a weed, what are flowers?"

Bob ran a little riff down from the E string.

She won't care that I am dead
She laughs when she sees my bald head

But still I wish that I could be
The one she sees when she does dream

"I do see you, Bob," Karen said. She hadn't moved her hands or arms. She was just lying there, talking at the ceiling. But she had moved her foot so that its sole was lying along Michael's calf. He like the long cool feel of her sole.

"I see you now and I see you in my dreams," Karen said. "I see you in my car and I see you in the hall playing your goddamn guitar." Michael looked at Karen and saw her close her eyes. "Michael's a nice man, Bob." She rubbed his calf. "You know that. He's kind and he's thoughtful and he keeps to himself. If every man in this world was a Michael it would be a better world."

"I wasn't worrying about his virtue," Bob said. "It's the man inside, like you said. The man who keeps to himself. I mean, Karen, you and I can both appreciate Michael, the kind of man he is, but does he ever get to appreciate himself? To get the benefits if you know what I mean? I've been listening to you two all night and I got to worrying about Michael. His soul, for example. Where does a man like Michael keep his soul?"

Michael thought it was strange to be lying under Karen's sheet listening to Bob talk about his soul. But somehow he didn't mind them going on this way. Maybe he didn't get the benefit of himself, who could say? They could talk about him all night if they wanted to. The him he kept to himself, his soul, his small knees and his big belly. It made him want to go back to sleep.

"Listen to this," Bob said.

One morning God woke up and spoke my name
Bob, He said, you know life's just a game
I said I knew it well
It's losers go to Hell
Bob, God said, that isn't what I mean

Bob stopped singing and looked as though he was listening to someone crying. With his face still turned away from the bed, he intoned, "I asked God what He did mean but He never answered me and I never heard His voice again."

Michael wasn't sure if this was supposed to be a talking part of Bob's song or if Bob really had heard God's voice. Sometimes, as a child, he had heard his own name spoken when he was alone, but it was always the voice of a parent or teacher calling him back to himself when he drifted away. Except one time he had been unfaithful to Lee-Anne when they still lived together and her voice sounded as though someone had a scarf around her neck and was strangling her. That was before he and Lee-Anne went to the place where they got undressed.

"Michael."

He had fallen asleep and Bob's voice came to him through a thick veil of dream.

"Michael, I was wondering if you could do me a favour."

Karen had rolled away from him and was sleeping in a tightly rolled ball.

"I need you to help me with something, Michael."

Michael sat up in bed. He was still wearing his cowboy shirt, unbuttoned, but the rest of his clothes were on the floor. He didn't want Bob to see him groping around for them.

"I'll meet you in the living room," Michael said.

"Make it the kitchen."

Michael sat up in bed while Bob stood up, slung the guitar over his shoulder, then, using his chair for support, scraped his way down the hall.

When Michael got to the kitchen, Bob was sitting in a wheelchair with a blanket folded around him. He turned his big head towards Michael and raised his hairless eyebrows.

"Gotta go outside, Michael. Whole world's outside. Now just grab hold of those handles and we'll scoot out the back door here."

On the other side of the kitchen door was a deck with a barbecue that gave off an odour of charred meat. Michael found himself thinking he would have expected Bob to be a vegetarian. There was only a sliver of moon, but enough light from the kitchen window that Michael could see the barbecue, the deck, a wooden ramp leading down to the grass.

"Down there," Bob said.

Michael tilted the wheelchair back, then rolled it slowly down the ramp. The rain from earlier in the evening had stopped but everything was still wet and the whole way down Michael could feel his rubber soles trying to slip. A block of wood was nailed across the bottom of the ramp.

"That's to keep me from running away," Bob said. Michael eased the big wheels over the crosspiece and onto the lawn. Pushing up beside the house was a thick weed maple. One of its branches lay damply against Michael's arm.

"Keep going for a bit," Bob said. "Out from under so we can see the sky."

Michael rolled the wheelchair along the grass. The ground beneath was bumpy and made his forearms tremble as he pushed. He wondered what it must be like for Bob.

"You don't have to stand up," Bob said. "There's a chair by the fence."

Now Michael saw the wire chair. He pulled it over beside the wheelchair but didn't know whether he wanted to sit on it. It was beaded with drops of water that soaked up the light from the kitchen and the moon.

"Take this," Bob said, unwrapping the blanket from his shoulders. "I don't feel cold."

"You will without it."

"I mean," Bob said, "I don't *feel* cold. No matter what the temperature. Here, take it. I'd like you to sit beside me. If you don't mind."

Michael accepted the blanket and spread it on his chair. He couldn't remember the last time someone had asked him to sit beside them. Although, just a couple of hours ago, Karen had asked him to lie down beside her—what he meant was that since he was a child and his father would pat his chair or the sofa to get him to jump up beside him, no *man* had ever asked him such a thing. He wondered if Bob reminded him of his father. Not on the outside. His father had been— still was—big and hairy. For a long time he'd managed an appliance sales and repair franchise. Then he'd owned it and their house had been the first on the block with central air conditioning. Whatever Bob used to do, Michael couldn't imagine him working in a place like his father's store.

"Great sky," Bob said. "I always like to come out and look at the sky after it rains. You ever do that?"

"Once or twice," Michael said, though he never had. But more than a few times he'd gotten out of his truck, if he was driving on a road with flat fields, and tried to spot the end of the rainbow. Sometimes he'd even tried to drive to where it seemed to be, just for something to do.

"What would you say the sky looks like?"

Michael looked up at the sky. There were still clouds along the horizon, but mostly there were wispy veils and stars. Was this some kind of test? It was as if he were a little kid again and he was sitting beside his teacher and he was supposed to come up with the right answer. In a way he wished he could, there was something about this Bob. He had the crazy idea of saying the sky looked like an upside-down half cantaloupe with the seeds falling out. "It looks like an upside-down half cantaloupe with the seeds falling out."

Bob didn't react. Michael closed his eyes and imagined himself under an orange sky with the seeds raining down. Then he had a picture of himself, Bob and Karen—him in his wire chair, Bob in his wheelchair, Karen in her bed but without the house, all under this glowing orange sky and its thick rain of cantaloupe seeds.

"I like it," Bob said. "I was afraid you would come out with some kind of bullshit about the black starry heavens, you know the kind of crap I mean."

"I guess so," Michael said.

"That kind of shit isn't in you. You don't have to avoid it, Michael, you're too pure to have it. Promise me you'll always be yourself. Cantaloupes, avocados, even a big jar of strawberry jam. You want to know what the sky looks like to me?"

"Sure."

"Holes. I look up there and all I see is all the empty spaces left by the dead people. Can you see them?"

Michael looked up at the sky. He couldn't see his cantaloupe but he couldn't see any holes either.

"Do you want to hold my hand, Michael?"

Michael got a bad feeling in his stomach.

"If you hold my hand you can see the holes."

"It's okay."

He was about to stand up when Bob's hand landed on his. He hadn't noticed Bob's hands before, they must have been hidden under the blanket, but this hand was big and strong, even strong enough to move appliances, and it settled on and surrounded Michael's hand as though Michael truly had shrunk down to being a child again.

"Do you believe in God, Michael?"

Michael hadn't been expecting this any more than he had expected Bob's hand. His father had always said there couldn't be a God or the world wouldn't be such a mess, but this theory brought no response from his mother, which meant she disagreed. "Why do we go to church?" Michael had once dared to ask, and his father had replied that it was good for the business and good for the soul.

"I don't know," Michael said. "I didn't think I had to make up my mind yet. I don't even know what God means."

"The big stuff, Michael, the forces outside and the forces within. Big cosmic currents. Stuff we don't even have a name for. In our culture we call it God."

Michael wondered what Bob meant by "our culture," and he was just asking himself whether he wanted to be part of it when Bob squeezed his fingers. Michael jerked his hand free and stood up.

Michael looked up at the sky. The darkness was beginning to leak away. His Jesus Was a Cowboy shirt felt thin and sweaty. He would have liked to be back in bed with Karen, but he knew that wasn't going to happen.

"Better go," Michael said. "Promised my sister's husband I'd help him out this morning." He looked down at Bob in the wheelchair. His pale skull was glowing, but the glow looked tired and worn out.

"You can wheel me out front," Bob said.

As Michael manoeuvred Bob's chair around the house and out the gate into the drive where his truck was parked, the light was starting to rise. The sky had turned grey-blue and the houses across the street were beginning to emerge like forgotten ghosts out of the darkness.

"It really was a treat to meet you," Bob said. Michael turned to the house, hoping to catch a last glimpse of Karen. She was sitting on the front steps, wearing the white blouse she'd had on when they met, top button undone, and she was smoking a cigarette and drinking a cup of coffee.

Michael wondered if he should go and kiss her goodbye, or wait for her to make the move. Even as he stood with his hand on the door to his truck he could feel the cool imprint of her sole against his calf.

"Come back soon," Karen said. Michael stepped into his truck and switched on the engine. It caught with a loud rasp that smothered everything but the sound of his tires crunching the gravel as he backed onto the street. The lines of emerging houses blurred into the heavy dawn mist he knew would be turning silver on the fields and over the water.

Mist and water were on his mind these days, because he was working on a rich man's house, half an hour from Kingston up the Fall River. *A rich man*, that's how Michael thought of Rich Chambers, because of the name of course but also because everything about Rich Chambers spoke richness. The wads of cash. The desk with its receipt pads, its cheque books, even its little strongbox built into one side which couldn't hold, Michael figured, anything much more valuable than the cash and jewellery that was carelessly left lying around the house.

Chambers had picked his land well. He had fifty acres of maple and willow woods at a place where the river took a squiggle and made itself a natural pond before narrowing into a long deep chute that swirled and foamed. The land sloped gently down to the water on both sides, and every morning when Michael arrived—having entered the property via an unlikely dirt road that led through a farm to this paradise that must once have been that farm's most treasured haven—he would push his truck door open, step out and stretch, relieved to be back.

The house itself was a low-slung sprawling pine-log-and-batten fantasy that combined, as Michael told his sister, a ye olde outside with some kind of dream appliance-and-tile interior that had turned into a nightmare. As Michael stood at his truck looking down on the house and past it to the river, he could almost blur out the thousand disaster details he knew about and imagine the fantasy working. Beautiful cabin in the midst of fragrant towering maples, the look and smell of water, the raw pioneer beauty of the Fall River enhanced by two dishwashers, imported Italian terra cotta tiles for the floors of the kitchen, the four bathrooms, the three fireplaces, air conditioning, a double-capacity septic system and a family room with its own ice- making refrigerator.

The rich man had a rich man's wife. Her name was Lucia and before Michael's father told him he'd heard she was the daughter of an Italian developer in Toronto, Michael had been unable to place this bony-faced woman with long blonde-red hair and fingers so loaded with rings you would think she must tinkle while brushing her teeth. Those teeth were large and white, which offended Michael's prejudice against large teeth, but her mouth was her best feature. Her lips were wide, soft, always curved in a smile with a tiny whiplash at the end, and when they just barely pressed together, which was how Michael liked them the best, and turned towards him as though she listened to his plans for the house with her mouth and not her ears, he felt a strange swirl inside himself, as though he was being rushed along those mysterious Venetian lagoons of which so many photographs and paintings were to be found on the walls and in the corridors of the house.

"Lucia Chambers," Rich had introduced his wife, and watched them shake hands.

"So you're the new architect."

"Not exactly," Michael said. "I just fix things."

"Like washing machines?"

"Sometimes."

"So you work for the new man," Lucia had said, a touch of frost in her voice, to let her husband know she didn't like being tricked into taking seriously the kind of person who should be coming in the service entrance, if only someone had thought of having a service entrance.

"He *is* the new man," Rich Chambers had said, clearly pleased with himself for having dug up such a genuine yokel. "It's only that he doesn't like to boast. Everyone says he can fix and do *anything*."

When he started working for Chambers, early in the spring, Lucia Chambers was often to be found downstairs. Now it was July, and aside from occasional sweeps to the kitchen for coffee or orange juice, little jaunts during which she always wore the same outfit, a black satin wraparound robe with clusters of yellow butterflies, she seemed to have retired upstairs.

On the Monday morning following his Saturday night with Karen, Michael arrived well ahead of his crew because he still hadn't decided exactly where to put the retaining wall for the terraced garden he was building out from the house to extend towards the river. He wanted it to be placed where it could get enough breeze to discourage the bugs, be close enough to the river that it could create its own little world of repose, yet still be in easy enough reach of the house that it would seem like an invitingly easy few steps rather than some kind of excursion.

He was just tracing a possible line for the retaining wall with his heel when Karen's red Datsun emerged from the woods and pulled up beside his truck. She had on jeans and a T-shirt with a bright scarf knotted around her neck that made her look pale and windblown. He wondered how she'd found out where he worked. Though it was no secret in town, he couldn't remember telling her or Bob.

"Your sister called my place looking for you," Karen said. "Wanted you to know the others won't be out until this afternoon because they have to fix the cement mixer."

That would be Sadie, all right. Whenever he got lucky she would worm it out of him, then try to contact the woman and find a way to put herself between them. For years she had declared Lee-Anne her "best friend." She had even proposed that he and Lee-Anne move in with her and Rajiit. Luckily Rajiit had come up with one of his crazy fake proverbs, something about a man who lives with his boss soon won't be working for him.

"She invite you to dinner yet?"

"Just lunch. Quite a place. You build this?"

"Nope. Just tidying up after."

He watched Karen as she surveyed the house, the work-sheds and garage, then finally let her eyes follow the land down to the river. You always wondered what someone else saw when they looked at things. He always tried to be sensitive to that. To look at a situation through a client's eyes and see what it was that ruined their view, what it was they wanted to be seeing. One person could buy a place next to a downtown parking lot and all he would worry about was where to put the garden. Another would be searching for nests of rare birds.

"I shouldn't have butted in this way," Karen said. "I guess I was afraid you wouldn't come back."

Michael had started towards the river. He thought they could sit on the rocks where he and Rajiit and the others ate lunch every day. Karen chose herself one of the best places, a grey tongue-shaped slab that extended from beneath an old willow out over the water.

"I thought I'd see you again," Michael said. He wasn't sure what he meant by this and wished he had come up with something more reassuring, but truthful. The real truth was that he didn't specialize in women.

"I don't want to be wasting your time here," Karen said.

The leaves were spilling light over her hair and shoulders. He wanted to reach out to her, but before he could start to close the space between them, she was gone. Moving up the hill towards her red Datsun quick and soundless while Michael, admiring without understanding the amazing manoeuvre she had just accomplished, watched her weave her way through the trees until she reached the clearing where she was parked. He stood to wave as she drove away. She put her arm out the window and waggled her fingers as though to confirm that everything was still on track, details to be announced at a later date.

After Karen left he went to the house to tell Chambers where he had decided to put the wall. The door was an elaborately carved slab of red cedar that Chambers had commissioned from a West Coast artist, but its knob was an Aztec sun god whose face you had to put in your hand every time you wanted to go in or out. Michael was the one who'd put it together: it had taken him the better part of a week to hang the door so that it opened and closed evenly, so snug and weightless Chambers had called him a miracle worker and made Lucia come down to marvel at his local yokel's latest magic.

Chambers was in the kitchen, spraying foamed milk and coffee from the espresso machine into a large cup. As he gestured to Michael to sit down, his cell phone rang.

After answering it, Chambers put his hand on the mouthpiece and asked Michael if he would mind taking the coffee tray up to Lucia in her bedroom. By the time he got to the stairs Michael could hear Chambers talking figures. The rich man was into the stock market; daily—sometimes more often—his broker would call and numbers would fly about like bad news from Pandora's box. More than once Chambers had offered to open an account for Michael, or just to tell him what to buy and when to sell. "Of course I don't want to put you out of business," Chambers had explained. "But if you want to make money, then money is the place to make it from. It's so simple but no one understands it. Money is like anything else—it's made out of itself. You can't make money out of things. Things are old. Instead of trying to make money out of things, you should just buy them."

Lucia was wearing her black butterfly robe and sitting up in bed, reading what looked to be a foreign newspaper. Beside the bed was a stainless steel intravenous tree. There were no bags attached, it just stood there as a reminder that two afternoons a week nurses came and dripped in medicine for whatever mysterious disease it was that she had, but whose name neither she nor Chambers had ever spoken to him. Michael wasn't going to ask.

"Thank you, Michael. You can set the tray down here." Lucia picked up a magazine to create a space on her bedside table. "Don't look so worried, I promise not to die on you." She gave him that smile he liked so much and her large dark eyes stayed, unwavering, on his.

The windows in the bedroom ran from knee height up to the ceiling and made the bedroom seem an extension of the outside. A tree house perhaps, or part of the maple tree from which a large bough curved across the top, framing the view leading down to the river. From this vantage point the water was glassy and smooth, as though it had been deliberately constructed as part of some still-life scene only Lucia could appreciate. The bedroom suddenly seemed larger and Michael wondered what it would be like to be in this room, this house, alone with Lucia. She would be wearing her black satin and her butterflies. The floor would be cool beneath his bare feet and with each step he would be aware of the wood, just as he would sense the silvery folds of darkness.

"Was that your wife who came to see you?"

Without realizing it, Michael had sat down in a padded armchair opposite the bed. Lucia's voice had an unexpected dry edge. Or maybe he had suddenly fallen asleep, or into the trance of her enchantment. He forced his eyes back to Lucia. She was sipping coffee-stained foam from her cup.

"Not my wife," Michael said. "Some kind of friend, I guess." He wondered what judgment Karen would make if she could see him now.

"Some kind of friend, that's nice."

She was playing with him. Michael pushed himself up, inclined his head forward slightly as though he were a faithful old servant requesting permission to return to his duties, then made his way out of the room.

"You like working for rich people?" Karen had asked him at the tavern and he had replied that rich people were the ones most likely to buy what he had to sell.

Now he was standing at the top of the stairs, his left hand resting on the polished walnut rail that slowly spiralled down to the light-filled hall where he saw Rich Chambers sitting on a bench, sliding his feet into his boots. Michael wondered what it would take for him to send another man to his wife's bedroom with coffee. Being married to Lucia Chambers, maybe. Or Karen. His own boots, muddy and cracked, were waiting by the door. He walked right to them, eager to get out, to invent the errand that would take him to town.

"Crew late?"

"Had to pick up a cement mixer for the wall. They might not make it because the mixer needs to be fixed."

"Be wanting a hand today?"

At first Chambers had seemed to think he should prove something, be out there working with the men sweating through the common labour as though these people were neighbours helping him out just as he would later help them. His face would turn purple and the hair on his shoulders quiver as though about to fall out. After an hour or two Michael would rescue him with some invented task, but he always made sure to ask him to eat with them, perched on the little group of rocks they'd found down by the river. All that was before Chambers had officially moved into the house, bringing his vans of exotic rugs and furniture collected from foreign lands, his cupboards full of clothes and dishes and glasses, Lucia.

"Don't worry about it," Michael said. "Today's pretty well lost." He checked his watch. It was eleven o'clock. "I'm putting the wall just past the dwarf apple tree." They were outside now, and he led Chambers towards the place he and Karen had found. Lucia would be watching, he knew. He wondered if she was curious about what they were saying or just observing them the way certain children, the kind of child she would have been, like to observe insects after turning over a rock or kicking apart rotten deadfall. "I'm going to make it out of fieldstones, like this." He picked a rounded granite fieldstone from the ground. It was flushed orange-pink on top, almost the colour of a cantaloupe that could rain seeds from the sky. Moist chunks of dirt clung to the bottom half. He hefted it from one hand to the other. "Maybe he'll kill him," he could imagine Lucia thinking. She would like the idea of men standing outside her window, planning to kill each other over her. Powered by the scent of blood, Lucia Chambers, the rich man's wife, would float to the winner like a falcon, her claws ready to close over the shoulder of her new master.

The ones I hurt
Are the ones I love
That's why they call me
Turtle dove
I crawl on the ground

I fly in the sky
I lay my eggs
Right in your eyes

The one who hurts me
Is the one I love
She treats me like
A rubber glove
She leaves me soaking
And inside out
Hangs me to dry
On the water spout

"That's not very nice, Bob. You make it kind of hard for Michael to come around. You want to make him think I'm trying to use the two of you to make a pair?"

Bob was in the hall again with his guitar. Michael was curled under the sheet, his head on Karen's stomach. As she spoke her belly bobbed up and down, like the sea, and his head bobbed with it. What a twisty life, Michael was thinking. He knew a rich man named Rich and a stomach bobber's balladeer called Bob.

Later they went out to the back yard, where Bob said: "If you ask me about the human heart, I cannot pretend to explain it. The mysteries of the cosmos, sure. It's all a question of energy. Just learn to put your head there. Millions of people are doing it all over the world. Did you know that?"

"I've seen it in the newspaper," Michael said.

Bob was in his wheelchair, this time keeping the quilt wrapped around his shoulders. Michael stretched out in a canvas lawn recliner with a bottle of wine between his knees. Karen was sitting at the top of the ramp with her own bottle of wine. Every now and then she'd chip in, "That's bullshit, Bob," or "Why don't you ask Michael what he thinks?"

"Wouldn't you like that, Michael, big energy highway running through your head?"

"My head's pretty full as it is," Michael said.

"What with?"

In fact Michael had been thinking how strange it was that once again he had come over to Karen's, made love to her in his lucky shirt, ended up outside listening to Bob, who used to be the same thing as her husband, spout off about the universe. But now another vision was taking shape with alarming speed. Almost highway speed. It was a vision of Bob in his wheelchair in Lucia's bedroom instructing her about the mysteries of eternity.

"You have to consider that the entire history of everything is just a hiccup," Bob would say.

"When you're married to that hiccup, you can't think about anything else," Lucia would reply. She would take Bob seriously and understand his true value. She would organize one of those nineteenth-century parlour groups Michael's great-grandmother had belonged to in Kingston, and Lucia would get other rich women to join her in worshipping Bob, the Voice from Afar. Instead of having a bottle of wine between her legs she would consume it intravenously. Bob would handle the whole situation with ease.

About halfway through his bottle of wine, Michael began to talk about Lucia, the way over the past few months he had fallen in love without really knowing until today, or maybe even right now when he realized not only was Bob the one for her, but that to Lucia Chambers Bob belonged to a real

world he himself could never aspire to join. Which might
seem like some kind of insult but in fact this knowledge had
come as a tremendous relief, somehow unburdening him of
Lucia while at the same time giving him an understanding
he couldn't yet put words to.

From this amazing outburst it was only a few steps to
the truck and then forty minutes later they were parked at
what Michael judged to be a suitably discreet distance from
the rich man's house.

By the time they had gotten Bob's wheelchair down to
the river, Michael was sweating heavily. He had brought
them to a little sand beach that was just upstream from
the house and hidden from it by a small fold in the land that
left what to a child would have seemed a cliff arching over
the water.

"Not bad," Bob admitted. Despite what he'd said the
other night he drew the quilt around himself and stared out
across the narrow river as though he was supposed to be a
seer searching the sea for signs of returning heroes.

Karen was collecting bits of wood to make a fire. It was
four in the morning, the air so still that when the flames
began to crackle and spit, they and the smoke rose straight
up, as though heaven itself was sucking them into its lungs.

"What happens if he finds us?" Bob asked.

"I guess he kills us," Michael said. "He told me he was in
the foreign legion."

After that they listened to the water for a long time, and
it seemed to Michael that as the fire died down and settled
into glowing embers, the sound of the water grew louder
and more complex, wrapping round him again and again,
each layer different than the last, until finally he turned towards Karen. She had been woven in with him by the water.

He took her hand and they stood up. Bob was still staring at the river, his head nodding to its swirly rhythms, and as Michael led Karen up past the little cliff he felt Bob giving approval to what they were going to do, whatever they were going to do.

About halfway to the house Michael pulled Karen into the shadows of a tree. The light in Lucia's bedroom was on, the window open; Lucia and Chambers' voices drifted across the lawn, as comfortable and lazy as butterflies in the sun.

"She was watching us this morning," Michael whispered.

Karen undid the top buttons of her blouse, placed Michael's hand at the cleft of her breasts. "You aren't my last chance," Karen said. "You're the only one."

Michael finished unbuttoning her blouse. He bent forward and with his tongue he traced the line from the base of her throat all the way down to where her belly met her jeans. He was kneeling in front of her and from his pocket he took out the gold ring he had bought downtown that afternoon. He put it on her wedding finger thinking this wasn't how he had planned things, in fact he hadn't planned anything at all let alone decided to make some kind of proposition and then her hands were in his hair drawing him close and he could feel the ring rimming his ear as he unbuttoned her jeans and his tongue that could never find the words to speak continued on its journey.

edward/
eduardo

1. International Trade

I KNOW A MAN who hijacked a Mexican plane in Ecuador. When he was caught, the Ecuadorean police traded him to Cuba. After a few years in the cane fields, he decided to return to Mexico and face his time in jail. Things went badly and he was tortured. His group kidnapped the American ambassador, then traded the ambassador back on condition my acquaintance be flown to Italy. A woman who admired his looks and excellent manners brought him into her fashion house and taught him certain intricacies about fabrics and tailoring. Meanwhile, in Mexico, government ministers changed. He came home and opened a boutique in the old city. Now he is a successful businessman, still moving with left-wing friends. Sometimes when he drinks tequila, his voice grows thick with nostalgia as he talks about the countries he has known.

2. Marriage

For his wedding to Claudia, Thomas bought a new black suit. He was twenty-eight years old, no debts except for car payments and an overloaded credit card. They met at a newspaper where they both worked: Claudia as a financial editor, Thomas as a sports reporter. When a new computer system was installed, Thomas became the liaison between the sports section and the system engineers. A year later Thomas was a software consultant making twice his old salary and back visiting the newspaper for a Christmas party. Claudia, glamorous in black and green, was drunkenly celebrating the end of a disastrous affair with, I should admit, me. Thomas, along with Claudia and several others, ended up at a restaurant. He spent an hour admiring the curves of her throat, the way her hair fell to her shoulders, the amazing way she had claimed to sober up by saving all her martini olives in a separate glass, then eating them at the end, popping them into her mouth voluptuously as though they were grapes.

"I'm a serious person," Claudia told him after he drove her home that night.

"Of course."

"What I want is a baby."

They were parked outside Claudia's apartment. Thomas was watching the way the street lights caught in Claudia's eyes when he realized she had taken one of his hands and was absently caressing it, as though it were a familiar pet. Her hands were fine and supple, radiated a warmth that was spreading from his fingers and palms through his whole body. He imagined himself in Claudia's apartment, his body given over to the care of those hands. He imagined himself in Claudia's bed, using his own hands to explore her body.

He imagined a crib in the corner of Claudia's bedroom. In the crib would be a baby sleeping peacefully under a warm and fluffy blanket. Every now and then, between bouts of making love, he and Claudia would bring the baby into Claudia's bed where it would lie between them and suckle contentedly at her full breasts.

3. The Truth (i)

There is a worldwide movement of truth commissions whose goal is to establish certain facts by digging up mass graves. Politicians, anthropologists, villagers, officials and bureaucrats from various organizations witness these events. There is shock, grief, morbid humour, note-taking. The hope is that public viewing of these past traumas will enable the poison to be expelled. One person told Thomas that such an eventuality is impossible, because the true poison is human evil. Thomas's own reaction was to think of a book he had read as a child: in it, the Day of Judgment was represented by a series of ghoulish illustrations showing the dead—semi-skeletons still miraculously wearing ragged clothes to preserve their modesty—coming up for air to face their Creator. Perhaps that is the missing ingredient these contemporary unburials require: God. Or perhaps God's insistent absence is what the truth commissions are required to establish.

4. Airports (i)

Airports have become the barometers of revolution. In airports, certain people claim, you can read a country the way

psychics read palms. The first time Thomas saw the Guatemala City airport was in 1985. He was with his wife, Claudia,
and their arrival was not the beginning of a touristic visit but
the climax of two years of trying to have a baby. During this
time, Claudia's desire to possess an infant had grown ever
stronger, but when the doctors informed Claudia that the
only place her eggs could be fertilized was in a laboratory
dish, she declared to Thomas she would rather adopt than
"enter into space-age bionics. Do you mind? If the doctors do
it, I would always be afraid they had used our spare parts to
put together some kind of Frankenstein." A modest number
of soldiers hung over the balcony watching as they cleared
immigration and customs on their way to find a taxi. In pre-
paration for this moment, Thomas had been taking Spanish
lessons for six months. "Leave it to me," he whispered to
Claudia as they climbed into the car, but when the taxi driver
spoke to him in English Thomas was unable to reply.

5. La Casa Grande

The baby trade takes place mainly at the Hotel de la Re-
forma, aka La Casa Grande. Once La Casa Grande was the
home of a president, though no one remembers his name:
it is an old-fashioned hotel that looks like what it is, a converted mansion suitably walled and gated. It also enjoys
three other distinctions: First, it is ten minutes from the
airport. Second, it is across the street from Ronaldo's, a
Mexican taqueria which on one wall has a sign proclaiming
PLEASE SPEAK SPANISH WE PROMISE NOT TO LAUGH. Third, it is
beside the American embassy, which makes for ease in
changing money and getting visas and other documents for

the babies and children who, for varying sums, are delivered to the waiting parents at the hotel after the necessary paperwork has been completed.

6. Losing

Once at a party I met Vargas Llosa, the Spanish-Peruvian novelist, as he was called in an article in *Prensa Libre*. He had recently declared his willingness to be president of Peru. He was wearing an artfully cut navy blue suit, his face was clear, almost translucent, his features perfectly carved. A tall gracious man with a beautiful and charming wife. Why would a handsome and world-famous novelist who has spent much of his life in comfortable exile want to be the president of Peru—a country known for its insoluble economic problems and its vicious civil war? Artists who have spent time in jail go into politics to make sure their release from individual suffering becomes a victory for all. Vargas Llosa, on the other hand, wanted a return to common sense. The most Utopian fantasy of all.

7. Tortillas

Warm, layered, wrapped in linen towels, presented in a straw basket. The key to a successful tortilla: achieve its eventual shape—round and thin—without working the dough too much. Beginners' tortillas, Thomas's for example, are lumpy irregular shapes that make real cooks laugh and remind him of his unsuccessful attempts to make clay animals when he was a child.

8. The Baby

When Thomas and Claudia got Eduardo, he was a small infant of indeterminate age. Eduardo was delivered by a slender man wearing sunglasses, a light-coloured plaid shirt, sharply creased brown trousers. Claudia had a bottle ready, as planned, and while she fed Eduardo, the agent told them a story about one of his parents' dogs, a bitch boxer named Kiki. Kiki used to be very jealous of the cat. Every time this cat, who had become pregnant, climbed into the lap of a family member, Kiki would crouch nearby on the floor, growling. One day, shortly after the kittens were born, Kiki snatched the cat out of the corner, carried her by the neck to the yard, then shook her to death.

"What a terrible story," Claudia said. They were sitting at a low table in the hotel's inner courtyard. Thomas and the agent were drinking Mexican beer; Claudia had a lemonade and soda drink that she'd taken up as dysentery insurance.

"No," said the agent, "it's a wonderful story. First my father threatened to kill Kiki. But we begged him to forgive her and as we begged we started to cry which made my father, who was always very sentimental, cry with us. By the time we had all dried our tears and forgiven each other, Kiki had begun to produce milk. She offered herself to the kittens, they began to nurse, she became their mother. It was the perfect adoption."

Thomas was noticing how the baby's skin, much darker than his own, seemed, in fact, to almost match Claudia's, who had one Italian parent. Eduardo had been the baby's name, but his papers now read Edward. There was even a certificate, stamped by a doctor sympathetic to the idea of foreign adoptions, attesting that Claudia had given birth to "Edward" while under his care.

"It is an amazing story," the agent said. "In fact the kittens grew up believing they were dogs. One of them even married the neighbour's dog."

"You had a ceremony?" Claudia asked.

"They did. Several times."

When the agent got up to leave, Thomas also stood. Edward was in Claudia's arms, sucking contentedly at the bottle of formula. "I wish you the best of luck," the agent said. "Also with the baby." There was, Thomas later thought he remembered, a movement of the agent's eyes toward the baby as though he was tempted to look at him one more time, possibly even pick him up.

On a return visit for reasons he could never have envisioned, Thomas would come back to La Casa Grande, sit in the bar, order a beer, try to reconstruct the scene. He would take the same chair he'd occupied before and then, on the pretext of fishing in his pants for a lighter, would stand up as he had on that night he and Claudia had received Edward/Eduardo from the agent.

Then he would turn to the place Claudia had been sitting. He would remember the way Eduardo's lips had compliantly shaped themselves to the rubber nipple. Remember wondering what the agent must have thought to see this baby in a foreign woman's arms, its mouth so happily attaching itself to this foreign source of nourishment.

"We'll do our best," Thomas said to the agent. Claudia didn't speak. Motherhood had carried her off into a new world of silent happiness.

Thomas walked the agent out to his car, a dusty black Ford, a model Thomas remembered from his childhood.

As he came back into the hotel Thomas heard a heart-broken crying. "Papa, Papa," the voice seemed to be calling. The hotel was full of babies and young children who had been delivered to their adoptive parents. In the lobby he passed a couple who had their infant in a stroller. Automatically he noted the couple was German-speaking, blond, and that their fairness made a stark contrast to the baby's dark skin and jet-black hair.

When Thomas entered the bar he saw that the strange wailing was coming from Edward/Eduardo. Claudia had gone stiff, her arms rigid angles as she held her new child away from her body.

That evening, as Thomas, Claudia and the exhausted Edward ate dinner in the hotel's courtyard restaurant, the German couple told them that several of their friends had adopted Guatemalan children and that they hoped these children would find in each other some sort of comfort or solace as they grew up together.

"Our child's mother was killed by soldiers," the German mother explained. "Her father is so grateful to us he didn't want to accept the money."

"Ours is almost the same story," Claudia said. "We're so lucky we can offer Edward a secure future. At least in Canada he'll never have to worry about politics or money."

Details of Eduardo's mother's death had been provided to Thomas by the agent. They had been too horrible to pass on. In any case they could be guessed. In return, Thomas had not told the agent the details of Claudia's obsessive need to have a baby, a need that had led her and Thomas to turn their lives upside down in order to possess, finally, Eduardo. That too, it seemed to Thomas, could be guessed by anyone wanting to know.

9. Protection (i)

Biologists say protection begins with the skin. Although it does allow for a certain amount of—could this be the term?—interpenetration. In and out. To say nothing of the mouth, the fingers, the anus, the sex organs, other orifices.

After they brought Edward home, Thomas became obsessed with protection. He acquired a car and a safe deposit box. Clothes, a chiropractor, eleven mercury amalgam fillings plus two porcelain. Eyeglasses, custom-designed inner soles, a charcoal grey suit bought to look acceptable in Japan. A house, a sidewalk to get to the house, two plastic shovels to clear the snow from its sidewalk, a new furnace to keep it warm, screens to keep out the bugs, a feeder to attract the birds, a stereo system to supply suitable music, a retirement plan to ensure he and Claudia would not be a burden to their adopted child because they, of course, had decided to take all burdens upon themselves.

10. The Truth (ii)

After Claudia married Thomas, an occasion to which I was invited but tactfully sent a gift of flowers instead of going, she called to say her heart would not be at peace unless we became friends. I will admit it was difficult for me to imagine Claudia's heart being at peace under any circumstances. Nonetheless, for old times' sake and because I was curious to see if marriage had changed her, I agreed to meet for tea in a restaurant. A month later the meeting was repeated. We drank herbal tea because Claudia said coffee and black tea stain the teeth, and I was able to consider, in the fading afternoon light of two different cafés, that Claudia still had the face of a beautiful woman, a woman whose beauty was entirely uncorrupted by the repose of serenity or inner peace. More than a year passed before I heard from her again. This time she wanted me to meet her new baby, Edward. She told me Edward's story and asked me to speak to him in Spanish. I sat with him in my arms at the tea room of the Four Seasons Hotel and told him a story I remembered about a donkey. He smiled blissfully as I related the brave little donkey's struggles as he climbed up and down mountains carrying Jesus to Jerusalem. The poor little donkey was staggered by Jesus' weight but found strength in a special song taught to him by a sympathetic angel. Edward snuggled into me, even as I explained that because I was Jewish I wasn't actually permitted to believe in Jesus, personally, but I liked the story because it showed the power of music. Also, I explained to Edward, it was so long since I'd been a baby myself, so long since my grandmother had sung me this song whose melody had burned itself into my brain, that I'd had to make up the words. Otherwise it was the real thing. *La verdad.*

11. Protection (ii)

On the second visit to Guatemala, seven years later, the soldiers in the airport mezzanine were sufficiently numerous, and their guns sufficiently threatening, that Thomas found himself looking at the tile floor for signs of mopped-up blood. The idea was that while Eduardo was at camp, Thomas and Claudia would discover the country of their adopted son. On this occasion Thomas and Claudia stayed in a fancy downtown hotel. One afternoon Thomas played tennis with the hotel pro. Surrounding the hotel tennis court, parking lot and gardens were a few of those men with machine guns who had also been an ominous sign at the airport. Nothing could have been more embarrassing for Thomas than to find himself in a situation where he required people with guns to protect his right to play tennis with a penniless professional.

Thomas liked it even less, two days later, when he and Claudia were stopped in the hills outside Antigua, made to get out of their car by people also bearing guns. They were on top of a small plateau with a classic view of the rolling valleys of the Guatemalan highlands. Tiny rectangular patchwork fields on either side. A village on their right, not far away. Volcanoes rising in the distance.

"They could have killed us," Thomas said afterwards. "Taken our bodies somewhere and buried them. No one would ever know."

"The rent-a-car company," Claudia said.

"They wouldn't care, they have an imprint of my credit card. They'd just keep charging us until the bank account ran dry."

"I'm more worried about our plane crashing."

"We're not on a plane."

"We will be," Claudia said. "Don't forget to buy insurance."

12. Protection (iii)

Edward also developed protection. Firstly the imperfect protection of his skin, modified by numerous scabs and pimples, to say nothing of track marks, piercings in his lip and one nostril—and no doubt many other traumatic events hidden by his second layer of protection, his clothes. Jeans frayed at the cuff, a salt-encrusted leather jacket, a pendant he told Thomas represented his sign, Aquarius. Like Aquarius he carried water: in a bucket with a rubber tool he used to clean windshields at traffic lights.

13. Kiki Again

After Eduardo ran away the first time, Claudia told me the story the agent had told her about Kiki—the dog who had killed a cat to become a mother. "Which is the worst part? That the agent was telling me I would kill to be a mother or that because of me Edward would think he was a dog instead of a cat? I've thought about this story every day for twelve years. I think it was a curse."

I agreed, but not to Claudia. I tried to reassure her that the agent was simply making conversation. In any case she hadn't even noticed the real worst part, which was how much everyone enjoyed watching the grotesque spectacle that Kiki and her children provided.

14. The Return

Thomas's third visit to Guatemala came after Eduardo had disappeared for good shortly before his sixteenth birthday. The police, the private detectives he hired, even Eduardo's friends from the street assured Thomas that his son would turn up again. Thomas's friends also assured him that Claudia's hysteria was perfectly normal, and that everyone knew they had given Edward every advantage and consideration.

When Thomas's plane landed, the airport mezzanine was empty of soldiers. Instead it was jammed with people waving and shouting to their relatives and friends. In his now much improved Spanish Thomas asked the taxi driver to take him to La Casa Grande, where he had made his reservation because, after everything that had and hadn't happened, he needed this final return.

Before his trip to Guatemala he had written to the village priest who had been his first contact in the adoption process. A letter had come back inviting Thomas to visit. The letter also promised the priest's help—however ineffective it might be—in researching Eduardo's past.

The evening of his arrival at La Casa Grande Thomas sat alone in the bar, trying to reconstruct—as has already been related—the exact details of that meeting when the agent handed over Eduardo to Claudia, thus beginning Eduardo's brief and unsuccessful existence as Edward.

The next morning Thomas drove to Antigua. There, too, he registered in the hotel where he had stayed with Claudia. He sat at the same table they'd used in the garden, took his coffee near the perch where two large parrots sat staring over the heads of the tourists, making sporadic derisive comments in a Spanish Thomas couldn't understand.

On his visit with Claudia, the central square and its surrounding arcades had been almost empty. Military vehicles had been stationed at every corner and aside from clusters of soldiers only a few dispirited pedestrians had been visible.

Now the square was thronged with tourists in khaki shorts and knapsacks, shoeshine boys, pedlars of blankets, trinkets, shawls, statues, knives, hats—anything that could be bought and carried. Even the bank was packed: Thomas had to stand in line for half an hour to get a traveller's cheque cashed. Afterwards he walked to a church where he and Claudia had lit a candle for Edward's safety. On his way he passed a cluster of stores advertising Spanish lessons and adventure vacations, cafés promising "typical" food, Italian-style coffee, bagels, even the use of Internet and e-mail facilities.

Thomas wondered what Eduardo would think of this place, then had a sudden and sharp desire to be here with Eduardo, to be drinking coffee with him in one of the new fancy cafés, to be walking down the cobbled streets together so he could turn to his son and see this particular southern light on his face. For a few minutes he tried—not for the first time—to convince himself Eduardo was indeed in Guatemala, was waiting to be discovered, was perhaps even watching him right at this moment as he stumbled towards the church.

The next morning Thomas took the road out of Antigua and followed it to where it joined the highway, at Chimaltenango. Most of the old town had been knocked down in the 1976 earthquake. Now the highway was lined by low concrete-block buildings with corrugated metal roofs. The traffic was antiquated dented cars, transports and packed buses emitting black clouds of diesel fumes, pick-up trucks often filled with farm workers or machine-gun-bearing soldiers, four-wheel-drive vehicles like his own. Every second building on the highway seemed to be some kind of car or metal repair shop. The rest displayed Orange Crush signs that extended into the tangles of sagging electric wires.

Along the crowded sidewalks everyone seemed to be in a hurry, though why or to where was unimaginable to

Thomas. As he left the town the number of people on the sides of the road diminished. Here the women balanced bundles of clothes or rugs or vegetables on their heads; the men had their bundles, usually firewood, resting on their backs, with a carrying strap passed across their forehead so they walked leaning forward, necks bulging with the strain. Some of the men, despite their burdens or even the fact that they were going up a steep incline, weren't walking but moved at a steady trot. Occasionally Thomas saw boys and men in soccer shirts loping up and down the hills, as though they were in training.

After a while he stopped at a large chalet-style restaurant apparently intended for tourists like himself. But aside from a few foreigners, the people inside seemed to be well-dressed Guatemalans, their children turned out in ironed shorts and frilly frocks. What, he suddenly wondered, did these children think when they saw the crowds of shoeshine boys in the squares of whatever city they came from, or the children kneeling in the fields, arms beaded with sweat and pesticide?

"So you came to see where it all began," the priest said. His white collar, as though it had never been worn before, gleamed from beneath his sweat-stained shirt. His face was dark and narrow, his nose a thin triangle supporting metal-frame glasses that sagged to one side.

They were standing beside Thomas's rented Jeep, now covered in dust after a spine-jolting ride over a two-kilometre dirt track that had taken him half an hour to navigate. The priest, as he promised, had met him at the church, a concrete-block rectangle with a cross in front. There were a few other houses, all built out of blocks, and across a tiny valley, a small cluster of wooden shacks.

"Too bad you couldn't have seen this place before. I came here the first time almost twenty years ago, when I was preparing to study. Then it was truly picturesque. The thatch roofs, the Indians in their costumes."

From where they stood they could see families working the tiny fields. A few children approached Thomas, one of them with beads hanging from her arm. They were barefoot and in shorts. It was easy to see they were half starved. Eduardo would have been one of these children. Or by now a shoeshine boy or working on the coffee harvest.

As they were talking the priest, pausing every few seconds to push his glasses up his nose, had walked him around the church to the back, where there was a small graveyard.

"Over here"—he pointed to a grassy corner—"is where the family lived. That was before this church was built. At that time, the graves were on the other side of the hill. The mother came from here, *una indígena*, the father was a Ladino, from a town on the coast. They met during harvest, he got her pregnant. He couldn't marry her but he sent her to live with his parents while she had the baby. After he was born she came back to live with her own family. When the army burned the village she was killed. This is her grave. No one knows what happened to the father."

15. Airports (ii)

Thomas gets back to La Casa Grande after dark. As always the hotel is filled by couples with or awaiting their new babies. The bar is closed, so he crosses the boulevard to Ronaldo's taqueria and orders a drink, eventually followed by supper.

By the time he returns to his room it is almost midnight. He telephones Claudia.

"So?"

"I went to his village and talked to the priest."

"And?"

"If Edward is here, he certainly hasn't gone back to his village. Or if he has, he doesn't want to see me."

"That's it?"

"Sorry."

In the middle of the night, Thomas's phone rings. The priest is on the line. He asks Thomas if it's too late to talk.

"Of course not," Thomas says.

"I'm in the lobby."

Thomas gets dressed. Now the priest is wearing a light plaid shirt, sharply creased brown trousers. His metal-frame spectacles have been replaced by sunglasses that sit squarely on his nose and hide his eyes.

"Sorry," the priest said. "I needed to meet you before we really spoke."

"You're Eduardo's father."

"Yes."

"I'm sorry about what has happened with Eduardo. I promised you we would keep him safe."

"Wherever he is, Eduardo will survive. He was always very strong."

"How old was he when we got him?"

"A little over a year. But he was small and just starting to talk. I said he was younger because I knew that would make it easier to find him parents."

"Can I ask why you sold him?"

Eduardo's father took off his sunglasses and looked at Thomas. For a moment Thomas was reminded of the time two weeks before Eduardo's definitive disappearance when he'd found Eduardo at the underpass where he was working and they'd gone into a restaurant for a coffee. Thomas was hoping, of course, that he would be able to buy his son some food. Or even convince him to come home. But Eduardo had accepted no more than black coffee and a package of cigarettes. Finally Thomas, partly for himself but mostly because he wanted to bring something back to Claudia, had asked Eduardo why he had chosen to leave their home and live this way. The boy had looked directly at Thomas, his eyes open and apparently candid. "I never had to ask myself that question," Eduardo finally said.

16. Airports (iii)

Thomas does not know how his story will end. He thinks his story is about a man who fell in love with a woman who wanted a baby. He didn't want the baby but he wanted the woman, so he agreed, which he knows was his sin. He is willing to be punished for the sin of being blinded by desire—but who ever said desire was good for the eyes? Also he is worried that although there was sin and there will be punishment, the connection might not be direct. Who will be the one to suffer? His wife? His son? Recently he read in a magazine about a woman who discovered, after going to more than a dozen doctors and trying almost fifty useless medications, that the cause of her asthma was the fact that in a previous lifetime she had been gassed in a Nazi concentration camp. Perhaps one day Eduardo will discover that the reason he has the wrong life in the wrong country is because his adoptive father wanted a lifetime of sex with his adoptive mother.

Suffering begets suffering but things were not always so bad for his son. Throughout his childhood Edward enjoyed playing Nintendo. At school he was a minor hero for a week after placing third in a city-wide cross-country race. But he never accepted long division. He hated arithmetic with a cold totalitarian zeal that made Thomas afraid he could eventually be hated the same way. Or worse, Claudia. When Edward begins to hate, Thomas would think, Claudia will be the target because she is the most vulnerable.

Perhaps, Thomas has even considered, Claudia could be thought to have brought her suffering on herself. In wanting to possess a child so badly she, too, allowed desire to blind reason. With her, as with Thomas, desire did not so perfectly convert to love.

The story could end with divorce.

The story could end with Eduardo returning to kill Thomas and Claudia in their beds. Or sing them songs. Or thank them. Or bitterly accuse them.

Or the story could end with the affair between Thomas and his latest Spanish teacher. "Why are you still here?" she asked him on the day he finally mastered the subjunctive. "To discover the mystery of my son," he replied. The following Monday, Thomas and his Spanish teacher disappeared into an airport, carrying backpacks, their shoes filled with enough traveller's cheques to start a restaurant in Oaxaca.

Claudia informed me of this sudden departure. Thomas had tried to keep his plans secret but the Spanish teacher, a Cuban with a conscience, as Claudia called her, had a dream in which she saw Claudia emitting rays of light like the

Virgin of Guadalupe and bleeding from her eyes due to Thomas's betrayal. She telephoned Claudia to confess all but Claudia surprised her—even relating the story to me she broke out laughing—by giving her blessing and asking the Spanish teacher to keep their conversation a secret from Thomas.

On the evening Thomas and his Spanish teacher left, Claudia and I went to the airport. We were able to see their airplane lifting romantically into the sunset while we sipped martinis and contemplated the vagaries of life.

Claudia then told me that, after grieving her child's departure, she had come to understand—at least in part—the story of Edward/Eduardo. The story was not, as she had long feared, a repeat of the story of Kiki with her playing the role of the boxer bitch. Nor was she a brave little donkey carrying Edward/Eduardo to a Jerusalem of safety and First-World prosperity. She had realized, Claudia said, that the story of Edward/Eduardo was not about Thomas or herself. It was not even a story she could possibly know—except for something about the ending, which was her secret to share or to keep. The secret was that, in the end, all of our lives would be footnotes Eduardo might or might not bother to seek out.

winter

THE FIRST LIGHT SCATTERING of snow on streets and sidewalks. The rustling of stiff newspapers blowing across frozen lawns. The pinched faces hurrying beneath the Christmas lights. But not Winter's. Winter happily sucked in the cold, acrid air. For the first time in months the world had snapped into focus. He felt vigorous, powerful, capable of believing in anything, even himself. Winter was, as Winter often said, Winter's season. Did people called May or June feel happier as summer began? Did Violets turn purple as their flowers came into bloom? Daisys yellow? Herbs green? Yes, no, maybe—Winter didn't care. All he knew was that the first touch of frost sent him into ecstasy, the first few snowfalls were so exciting he would wake to the soft sound of it at night, leap out of bed to watch the white stuff spreading its good news, often even as a grown and more-than-grown man stand outside for hours in those first snows, taking on its fortifying layers the way sun-lovers rush to strip off their clothes and begin sizzling their skin.

A half hour later, he was delivering a lecture on *The Return of the Native* by Thomas Hardy. "*The Return of the*

Native, by Thomas Hardy," he began. Thirty-two faces looked his way. This was downtown Toronto. This was multi-cultural, multilingual, multilevel education. These were thirty-two people in need of his course in order to gain their high-school diploma and therefore advance one more rung on the socio-economic ladder—a ladder of which everyone officially denied the existence because all were equal, but in fact a ladder whose existence was the only reason for the rapt attention awaiting Winter's next words.

"Thomas Hardy was one of the most important male British novelists of the nineteenth century," Winter announced. Or admitted. The weather in the room changed. A light blur fell over most of the faces. Some turned to stare out the window at the snowy night. "Like Canada's Margaret Laurence, another great writer in the realist tradition, Thomas Hardy was subjected to numerous attacks on his prose fiction because of its allegedly sexual nature." Heavy disinterest spread like black treacle through the air. "How many people here have read a book by Margaret Laurence?" Winter asked. A man near the back put up his hand. "What book was that?"

"*Lady Chatterley's Lover*," the man said, grinning. His name, Winter knew, was Alberto Silva. Alberto Silva rubbed his hands together.

"What was it about?" Winter asked.

"Sex!" Silva called out triumphantly. The class laughed. "It was hard feminism," Silva added. "That's what got it banned."

Later that evening Winter went to the tavern on Clinton, as he usually did on Tuesday nights, to have a few beers with some of his fellow teachers. He told the story of the student who had confused Laurence with Lawrence, how instead of correcting him he had waited to see if anyone in the class knew the difference. As he was telling this story he became aware of a contemptuous tone in his voice, a tone that he recognized as the currency of these gatherings but which he disliked himself for using, an ironical tone of superiority towards his students, as though they were just a wriggling subhuman mass whose every attempt to crawl into the light was bound to be met by comical failure.

The real subhuman, and he knew it, was himself. He was nothing more than an old-fashioned obsolete parasite feeding off their need to learn. When they finally seized power he and the other teachers would be discarded and left to wander the streets begging for handouts. Except for Leon Philips. Leon had abundant sandy hair heavily flecked with dandruff. Also, according to him, an ever-burgeoning portfolio of blue chip and computer-oriented investments that would make him a millionaire within two years. At night he taught and during the day he read the financial pages and made brilliant charts, master moves. Twice a week he spent the afternoon at the stock exchange, dressed in a three-piece pinstriped suit. Today he was still in uniform.

"False consciousness, as usual," Leon declared. He taught psychology and had even, for two years, undergone a psychotherapy whose details he used to recount at these evenings until being cured had enabled him to substitute the stock market, an undertaking for which his amazingly acute insights into the human condition had prepared him much better, he explained, than dreary courses in economics. "In fact, the only reason you asked the question was to validate your own status. The proof is that if you'd been intending to educate them, you would have corrected him."

Vivian Keller, a relatively young and recent addition to the drinking group, looked inquiringly at Winter. Bernard

Winter to be exact, but everyone called him by his last name. Winter, unused to being so much the centre of attention, felt he should defend himself.

"In my class we emphasize life experience," Vivian Keller said.

The man sitting beside Winter, a journalism teacher who had once informed Winter that the way to get women into bed was simply to take them home from gatherings such as this and ask them, point blank, leaned forward and said dolefully, "Ah yes, life experience," which drew general laughter and got Winter off the hook.

As was his custom, Winter left just as the others were loosening up, left with a small wave and a bill on the table. Outside the wind had picked up, the snow was driving into his face as he walked towards his apartment. When he took a deep breath the cold pinched his nostrils, tickled the insides of his lungs. His notes and books were stuffed in a dark canvas knapsack that swung easily from his shoulder. All those details. All those layers of politics, expectations, truths and deceits. When he got home the knapsack would be shoved into the closet. He loved going to bed knowing that even if he awoke in the middle of the night his books and notes were safely hidden away. He realized he was whistling; he was standing at a stoplight, the snow blowing into his face, and he was whistling.

Light spilled in the large second-storey window, flowed across the room to the doorway where Winter stood, examining the scene.

The scene was two empty chairs with a coffee table between. Earlier that morning the coffee table had been wiped clean of its little dust carpet, and for a while Winter had thought he would keep the table empty until it was time to serve coffee. Or perhaps coffee would not be what was wanted.

In any case, Winter had decided—whether coffee would be required, whether or not his guest would even consent to sit in one of the empty chairs—that there was something threatening about an empty table. As though it were a page waiting to be written on, a contract whose details must be determined.

Thinking about what "the contract" might be, the idea that his life could be seen like this, depressed Winter. "We can't have that," he said aloud, wandering back towards the kitchen for a drink. The apartment was a second-storey walk-up above a religious bookstore, and it was amazingly clean. Winter had lived there for the eight years since he had left Helen. Most of the last two weeks had been spent cleaning and organizing. Walking from the living room, which looked out onto the street, back past the two bedrooms and bathroom towards the kitchen, which looked out onto the metal fire escape that led down to a back lane filled with garbage cans and illegally parked cars and vans, Winter couldn't help admiring how sane and wholesome his apartment now appeared.

"The secret," Winter had confided to a friend the other night, "is giant green garbage bags. You buy a package of ten and tell yourself you can't have a drink until they're all full and in the street."

He'd exaggerated. A mere six giant green garbage bags had been all that was required. When he was done, Winter stood at his living-room window, looking down at them on the sidewalk, surveying them as though they were lumpy recruits presenting themselves for inspection. "Well done,"

Winter said. "At ease." The telephone rang. Helen. She was still out there. To hear her voice you'd think she'd been alone on an island forever. He told her so. "You wouldn't know what it was like to have a heart, would you?" she said. Then: "I take that back. You feel bad, all right. But you don't want anyone else to know it."

Winter was a tallish man, early fifties, at first sight all sinew and bone. He had a high, domed forehead, and he combed the remains of his black hair straight back, with small licks sometimes curling over the tops of his ears.

On the once-empty table between the two empty chairs he'd put, instead of a contract, a carefully slightly disordered newspaper, an ashtray, a few books. Travel books he'd chosen because they would provide good excuses for conversation. "So you're the kind of person who goes places," he could imagine hearing. There was a statement about money, about shallowness, about the privilege and desire to amuse oneself. On the other hand, if he put nothing on the table it would be empty and emptiness was something he had already decided to avoid.

Helen had wanted to have dinner with him. At least that had been the official excuse for her call, though Winter was convinced that the real reason she telephoned him every week was to make sure good fortune had not paid him an unexpected visit. He knew that she wasn't really trying to get him back, that she didn't even want him back. His theory was that she liked the occasional dinner to confirm that indeed there had been something big in the middle of her life. She needed that because, he had another theory, she saw life as a pointy egg lying on its side. You started at one end, infinitesimally small and young. Gradually you swelled until, mature, you grew positively round with experience. "You are the man of my life," Helen had told Winter a week after they started sleeping together. Despite everything, she had stuck to that story. Now that her life was moving towards its nether point she liked to look back on the moment of perfect roundness. Or so Winter theorized.

He had a thousand theories, maybe a million, most of them forgotten as quickly as they were invented. "You know, I have a theory," he would say to Helen, especially near the beginning, and she would smile and say, "Tell me."

"Tell me," she would say and Winter would feel as though he was stepping into a spacious arena, the giant benevolent chamber of his brain—a well-lit nuclear-powered workshop capable of manufacturing the universal range of ideas. Of course he didn't tell Helen about his brain and everything it could do because, at the time, he believed it would be unlucky. Then gradually his image of his own brain evolved to that of a second-hand bookstore filled with volumes no one would ever want to read.

When the knock at the door came, Winter was at the kitchen sink, running water over the frozen mass in the ice cube tray.

The woman standing there was shorter than Winter, but barely. Like Winter she had a gaunt stringy look, but her face was longer and with a sadness Winter had never seen in himself. "You look like I thought you would," she said, no sentimental gawking and when she took his hand he saw their palms and fingers were almost identical. "Cold hands, warm heart. Are you going to invite me in, or what?"

Beside her was a hard green suitcase with a pebble finish. Winter bent to take it. "I've carried it this far," said Doreen. "I'll manage the rest of the way."

Winter showed her her room. It had been his "office"—
junk room might be the better term—but in honour of this
visit he'd moved everything out, bought a bed and dresser
at a yard sale. Even painted the walls. Only yesterday he
had decided to add the finishing touch and he had spent the
morning at the Bay, trying to decide between a yellow and
a pink chenille bedspread. Pink had been his first choice,
the obvious one. But then he'd thought Doreen might be
offended by something so babyish, immature, reminiscent
of all the things she'd put behind her. That left yellow, since
the pale green they offered in that price range looked like
some putrid kind of soup. Yellow, Winter had considered,
was both feminine and dignified. He chose it and was having it wrapped up when he remembered yellow was the
colour of the daffodils they always sold to raise money for
cancer.

"Nice bedspread," Doreen commented, looking at the
pink chenille that Winter had stretched into place with military precision.

"It was that or green," Winter said, "they only had the
two colours."

Doreen turned to him and smiled. Everyone always used
to say that spending so much time together had made them
look alike. Winter wondered if his smile still resembled
Doreen's, which was wide and ever so slightly mocking.

Doreen set her suitcase down on the bed. "I like it," she
said. "It's very sweet."

"You don't think it's strange that she's there?" Helen asked.

"Why shouldn't she be?"

"Coming back like that. After we—"

"It's been eight years."

"She could have stayed in a hotel. She's a doctor, isn't she? She must have money."

"A research doctor," Winter said. "And I'm happy to have her as my guest. It's exciting to have a guest."

There was a sharp intake of breath at the other end, as though Winter had just led a brass band through Helen's office, celebrating yet another shocking infidelity.

"You never invited me," Helen said.

"You have your own place," Winter said.

"And if I moved out? What if I were homeless? Would you take me in?"

"Don't move out," Winter said. "You like your house. Mine's a dump."

"That's true. I wouldn't want to live there. How can Doreen stand it? She must spend all her time cleaning."

"She spends her time at the library. That's why she's here."

"It isn't fair. I was supposed to be the big love of your life. Now I'm just . . . an intermission between your teenage romance and the golden years."

"I've got to go," Winter said. "Don't you have work to do?"

"I'll do it later. While you're dining by candlelight or whatever old sweethearts do."

But most of Winter's evenings were reserved not for candlelight dinners but for teaching his night courses in English literature at the local high school. It was an honourable profession, low on financial reward. At an earlier era of his life, the fat part of the egg, he had been a university lecturer writing the definitive biography of Charles Dickens. In those days, when he'd lived with Helen, his office had been not a junk room but a study, a book-lined, walnut-desked, lead-windowed sanctus sanctorum in which he would sit smoking his pipe and surveying the ever-increasing piles of books, file cards, photocopied articles, binders of research notes that were being force-fed into the nuclear-powered benevolent chamber of his brain in order to emerge a stylishly written, elegantly comprehensive account of the life of England's and possibly the world's most famous novelist.

The brain had a different plan. Swallow the material it would, but instead of synthesizing, it incinerated. The more Winter read about Dickens, the less he knew. After a certain number of years even the names of Dickens' most famous works began to escape him. Of course they were on the tip of his tongue, he knew them as well as he knew his own mother's face, as he once said, though in fact that also had slipped off the edges of his vision.

"Stress," his department chairman pronounced soothingly. The book, his thesis, his financial future and his security in the ivory tower were all wrapped up in this one project. "Take your time. Everything passes." Then the chairman passed. Away. He was replaced by a distinctly less friendly presence, a fiercely ambitious woman with two doctorates, eighteen books to her credit, and a sour view of lazy white male professors who took without offering. Winter decided on the sensible path of salvation: he attempted to seduce her.

Winter was sitting in his kitchen, a cookbook from which he was copying a list of ingredients, spread out on the table when Alberto Silva, the Lawrence man, telephoned him.

"Dr. Winter?" Alberto began.

It was so long since anyone had called him doctor that Winter's first reaction was to say he had the wrong number.

"I recognize your voice," Alberto said, as though Winter had been trying to fool him. At which point Winter recognized Alberto.

"Mr. Silva?"

"That's me."

"How are you, Mr. Silva?"

"Not so good."

The familiar rumble of Silva's voice sounded thick and awkward over the telephone. Silva was in some indeterminate zone between youth and middle age. His invariable uniform was a grey suit with metallic threads that gleamed under the fluorescent lights. With the coming of the cold he had added a red V-necked cardigan, a red scarf and a beret that looked as though it had been stolen from a movie about Paris in the 1930s. Silva's wife, whom Winter had been introduced to once as he was leaving the class for the tavern, ran a Portuguese community newspaper. Silva, who said he was on disability because of a construction accident, was studying for his diploma so he could get a job as a baseball reporter.

"How can I help you?"

"You can't," Silva said. "I am calling to say I won't be coming to class any more because my wife is having cancer treatments and I have to stay with the children in the evenings."

Winter sat down, his heart thumping as though he himself had been diagnosed. Silva's wife: a roundish bright-eyed woman whose face had seemed, at least in memory, to glow with its own inner energy and purpose. Like Silva, she had been wearing a black beret. He realized he was having trouble breathing. "I'm very sorry to hear that," he finally managed. "Is she?—I hope—"

"I don't know," Silva said heavily. "I better go. She's coming home soon and she doesn't like to hear me talking about it on the phone. It makes her think everyone's talking about her funny, she told me."

"Wait—you don't have to quit the course. You can miss a few classes. I'll help you make it up later."

Silva didn't answer.

"I'll call you in a week or so. I'll bring the material to your house. Hey, look, Mr. Silva, a man who has read *Lady Chatterley's Lover* can skip a few classes. What do you say? I'll call you next week?"

"Okay," Silva said, and hung up.

Winter put down the telephone. Aside from Helen, he had few callers who required more than a few words of conversation. Now his ear felt as though it had been stuck to his head for a long time. He knew he had not handled the situation with Silva very well—and the idea that just a few nights ago he had been joking about the man's intellectual capacities when in fact he was dealing with a terrible tragedy only made him wish he'd been able to persuade the poor man that he wouldn't be penalized for his wife's illness. He wondered if that was how his students saw him— so strict and inhuman that the least deviation would cost them their chance at a better life.

The telephone rang again. He picked it up, expecting Doreen with some change in their arrangement. "Bernard Winter? This is Vivian Keller speaking. Do you have a moment?"

Winter sat down. His telephone was in the kitchen because having it in the bedroom had seemed vaguely obscene or maybe just too hopeful and the thought of it in the living room, glowing as a mute reproach to the non-existence of his social life, had been too much to bear. In the kitchen, it seemed to him, the telephone was just another utensil, like a frying pan or for that matter the pressure cooker, which he used even less frequently—never at all to be exact—though he'd bought it with the intention of improving his cardiovascular system with fish and vegetable dinners.

"Sure," he said, as though he always spent the morning on the phone, "what's up?"

"Well, Professor Winter—"

"Please don't call me professor, Miss Keller, I'm just an ordinary teacher, like you—"

Vivian Keller laughed. It was a pleasant sound over the telephone, a velvety chuckle he'd never heard at the tavern where, it seemed, she was always anxiously defending some politically fashionable point of view that all the other teachers looked down on.

"But I always think of you as Professor Winter."

"Just call me Bernard. Or Winter, like everyone else."

"Then you must call me Vivian."

"Right," Winter said. He had suddenly realized that in this conversation, as in the one with Alberto Silva, somehow everything had become turned around and he was the one who was supposed to think of something to say. But he had nothing to say. There was a little silence.

"Well, Bernard," Vivian said, "I was calling for two reasons."

Winter wondered what they could be. Even one seemed too many. There was another little silence, which began to grow long. Winter decided not to interrupt. This was Vivian's call, after all. *You go ahead, it's your nickel*, he recalled an old university friend saying, back in the days when he was still a professor, after it turned out that seducing his department chairperson was not the solution to his problems and he was phoning around about other job possibilities. As the silence evolved from long to awkward he imagined himself telling Vivian Keller it was her nickel. He decided not to.

"I thought they were very unfair to you in the tavern the other night," Vivian Keller finally resumed. "I know how hard it must be for you to teach at this level and I think your students ought to be . . . honoured."

Winter blushed. He felt humiliated—as though he'd been caught—well, he had been caught, caught talking as though he was better than everyone else.

"I was in the wrong," he said. "Believe me, I know it."

"I am honoured," Vivian Keller continued, as though she hadn't heard. "Believe me, you're a real inspiration."

Winter was sweating. His telephone was burning and pulsing and dancing as though it had been injected with some strange amphetamine. He was about to apologize again, then realized he was feeling not apologetic but angry, when Vivian Keller took up again.

"The second reason I was calling—well—I was offered free tickets to the new Ariel Dorfman play at the St. Lawrence Centre. Have you seen it?"

Feeling guilty for thinking her compliments were meant as insults, Winter explained that although he hadn't seen the play, he had heard it was marvellous—in fact he had seen only one review of it and couldn't remember what it said—and that he was looking forward to her account of it.

"I would like," she said formally, "to ask you to come with me. The tickets are for Friday evening. I have a meeting downtown in the afternoon and we could meet in the lobby beforehand."

Now both of Winter's ears were red. Doreen had already warned him she would be busy Friday evening, at a lecture on dissolving bones, and she had made it clear she didn't expect Winter to accompany her. Winter could hear Vivian Keller breathing anxiously at the other end of the line. He thought of Alberto Silva, at home with his stricken wife. "That would be very nice," Winter said. Vivian Keller's breathing slowed. When they had fixed the exact details, Winter put down the telephone and fled the kitchen.

Doreen's door was shut. Since her arrival, he had taught every evening. He would come back from class, Doreen would be sitting in the living room reading, they would have a glass of wine. At university they had always spent their evenings together. A couple of hours in the library, then back to the apartment Doreen shared with three other girls. "Mum and Dad," the girls called them. Twin beacons of good behaviour and hard work. They would drink tea and work on their essays until midnight, when Winter would go back to his own room. Except Saturdays when he would stay for the night. At first they just necked, groped, etc. In grade eight, Doreen had taken a pledge to remain a virgin until she was married. Since they were planning to marry when they graduated it didn't seem so long, at first. Eventually it did. They started having sex but Winter still stayed at Doreen's only one night a week because they didn't want to impose on her apartment mates and they couldn't afford to move in together.

In those years Doreen had luxuriant dark hair, a smooth but somehow severe face that broke easily into a smile that always hinted at forgiveness—although what she was forgiving wasn't always clear—large dark eyes with a disconcerting way of suddenly shifting away, as though towards an unexpected future. Afterwards Winter realized that sex had probably been a mistake. They both wanted it, but in all Doreen was more comfortable dressed than naked, more comfortable in a chair than lying awkwardly transfixed, condemned to silence because just a thin wall away her roommates were cuddled up with their teddy bears.

Things got too awkward to continue. Yet how to end? Most nights they continued as they had for three years, "Mum and Dad" drinking tea and writing essays that would come back with high marks and laudatory comments. Doreen, despite the pained martyred look that inscribed itself on her face during their weekly ritual, still spoke hopefully of marriage—as though it were a lifeboat that would eventually come to her rescue. But the prospect of them inflicting this kind of damage on each other hundreds of times a year was unbearable to Winter. He couldn't simply say to Doreen that they were making themselves miserable every time they took off their clothes, which would be the ultimate reproach and insult. The only logical solution was for him to be unfaithful then confess; Doreen would send him away and they would both be honourably released.

Having an affair turned out to be less painful than Winter had anticipated. After an evening of "Mum and Dad" he would go to meet his illegally beloved at a bar they'd taken up in common, then it was back to her apartment. How trivial the pleasures of the flesh! But how essential! Gazing up at the ceiling at the passing lights, Winter would try to feel guilty, to imagine the speech he was going to make to Doreen, etc. Winter grew so distracted by the

unexpectedly happy dialectic of his life that a theory viewing life as necessarily dialectical and therefore bigamous
burgeoned in his nuclear-power chamber until suddenly it
was four months before the big wedding and Doreen was
talking about sending out invitations, arranging bridesmaid
dresses for her roommates, and who was Winter going to
have as his best man?

Winter panicked. After three days of relentlessly torturing himself to come clean he finally told Doreen his
father was having a hemorrhoid operation the Friday before
their planned Sunday wedding, and that the marriage, since
it couldn't be advanced, should be postponed a few weeks.

"Hemorrhoids," Doreen said speculatively. At this moment in her life she didn't yet know that her disappoint-
ment with Winter would lead her to decide to go into
medicine. "I hope they're not hereditary."

"Doreen is obsessed with the wedding," he told his other
girlfriend that night. Her name was Phoenicia but she called
herself Fenny. She herself was engaged to a very handsome,
rich and absent naval-officer-in-training. "I'm just using you
to keep myself sane," she had told Winter the first night.

"I thought you wanted to marry her," Fenny said.

"I've changed my mind."

"You'll get over it."

"No, I won't," Winter said. Then: "I'd rather marry you."

"But I'm taken."

Winter was hit hard. He'd never expected to propose
to Fenny, but now that he had, it was obviously the perfect
solution. He wouldn't marry Doreen because he would
have already run off with Fenny. How could she refuse?
After everything they'd shared together, how could she
want to be with someone else?

"Don't you like the way we—"

Fenny put her hand on his mouth. Then she lay on top of him, the way Winter liked. "It's just sex," she said.

Winter opened Doreen's door. Like metal filings jumping to obey a powerful magnet, every object in Doreen's room now obeyed the call of order. The pink chenille bedspread was stretched taut enough to split at a razor's touch. Her green pebble-grained suitcase was open and showed two small stacks of perfectly folded clothes. Her toilet articles had been arranged on the dresser in ascending order of height, from the lowly cylinder of dental floss through the box of bandages and the deodorant stick to climax at a bottle of eau de cologne. On her bedside table was a small stack of magazines topped by a paperback book: *UFOs: The Untold Story*.

Winter wondered if he should attach particular significance to her leaving the book so obviously displayed. Was Doreen trying to tell him that she now believed herself to be an alien? Winter closed her door, continued on to the living room where he stood at the window and looked out at the street. The fat part of the egg was over, but egg—yes, there was still a lot of egg left. Helen was right: it was somehow bizarre that Doreen had come to set up camp with him again. And they were the way they used to be, "Mum and Dad," sitting in this room at night, sipping wine instead of tea, him marking papers while Doreen studiously read. Come Saturday night would they go to bed the way they used to? Winter tried to imagine this. It wasn't so difficult. With a little practice they could probably learn to get through it, possibly even enjoy it. Perhaps the whole dialectic was offering itself again: maybe that was the real meaning of Vivian Keller's phone call. Winter tried to imagine being in bed with Vivian Keller. Her voice would be throaty and full, her skin lush and fragrant. They would have a good time. It would just be sex, but that might be an extremely welcome change from its absence.

Winter sat down. Somewhere, Alberto Silva was with his wife, worrying about her illness, the fate of their young children, possibly even the strange event of his night-course teacher offering to help him. In front of Winter was the file folder with his students' records. He took out Alberto Silva's page. Silva had registered late, mid-October, and had not yet handed in either of his two assignments. He'd been excused from the first one because of his late registration, and had asked for an extension on the second saying his computer had crashed just as he was completing a second draft. To prove this he'd shown Winter the first page of his first draft, of which Winter had approved the plain and error-free writing. "This looks good," Winter remembered saying. "I only want to show you my best," Silva had replied.

Now Winter saw Silva's address. His house was only a few blocks away. There was a series of Thomas Hardy poems Winter had xeroxed to distribute at the class. He put a set in a brown envelope marked with Silva's name and address, then started out for his house.

He'd gone out early in the morning for milk. It had been grey and cold enough to redden his hands just crossing the street. Now the sun had burned away all but the last layers of clouds. The crusts of snow on the sidewalk were melting and people were walking with their coats undone.

Silva lived on a short residential street. His house was small, a two-storey brick house with a Christmas wreath on the door; on the lawn a half-completed snowman. Instead of a proper mailbox Silva had a small metal-clad opening in the door. Folding the envelope to slide it in, Winter was so carefully avoiding the wreath that he somehow lost his balance and his elbow banged against the door. As though he'd been standing there, Silva opened it immediately. Winter, embarrassed, held out the brown envelope to explain himself.

"Since you weren't coming to class I brought this around," Winter said.

"Thank you," Silva said, though as he stood blocking the doorway he didn't look particularly grateful. Instead of his dilapidated grey suit, he was wearing slacks and a shirt in which he seemed—Winter couldn't exactly decide how—different than usual.

When he got home the telephone was ringing again. This time it was the secretary of a certain Mr. Peters at the "Night School Evaluation Unit" of the Board of Education, to ask if he might meet with Winter that afternoon at his office.

"Night School Evaluation Unit?" Winter repeated. He'd never heard of such a thing.

"It was established by the Ministry last year," the secretary replied. "Part of the budget redistribution process. No one's heard of us, it seems. When I telephone to arrange Mr. Peters' appointments, some of the teachers think it must be a prank call." As she said this she laughed and Winter laughed too because, of course, that was exactly what he had been thinking. Although it did still seem to him quite bizarre that his telephone had rung four times in one morning. At least this conversation was relatively painless.

"I'd be delighted to come," Winter said, "but would it be possible for next week?"

"I know, I know, it's such short notice," the secretary sympathized. "I was originally scheduled to call today to ask you for two weeks from now. But Mr. Peters has to go out of town next week, and the following week he has just been asked to replace Margaret Atwood as the featured speaker at a special session on Canadian Culture at the American Languages Association in New York, and he was *so* eager to see you, he wondered if it might possibly be convenient..."

As it turned out, Alberto Silva was some kind of "undercover agent." "At least that's what they call themselves," Mr. Peters explained. He was nattily dressed in a blue suit that showed red suspenders through the open jacket. His face was round, his smile toothy, and to begin with he told Winter that he was Chinese, from Hong Kong, and a great admirer of Canadian multiculturalism. The framed diplomas on his wall included a Master of Business Administration degree from Harvard University.

"What we're concerned about is the quality of education," Mr. Peters said. "And I don't mean letting down standards if that's what you're afraid of. Believe me, I pride myself on being old-fashioned." He gave his wolfish grin. "Our intention is to eventually check every single teacher in the system. Although it seemed sensible to start with those closest to retirement."

"Retirement?—I haven't any—"

"Of course," Peters said, flipping open Winter's dossier, "you're with us on an annual contract. Either you or we could terminate at any point."

"I had no plans," Winter said.

"Nor did we. We were simply... well... you must

agree Mr. Winter, certain teachers who *are* near retirement might be eager to step aside. And then, after Mr. Silva's first few weeks in your classroom, there was the complaint, so we decided—"

"The complaint?"

"Another teacher, actually. Which is most unusual. She said, and although I sympathize with this remark, Mr. Winter, please don't think I take it as a criticism, that you appear to favour, let me quote, 'narrow-based achievement over life experience.'"

Winter flushed. There was a union that docked every one of his paycheques. That would be something to investigate after this meeting because when he was "terminated" he intended to sue for a settlement.

"We're not entirely dissatisfied with you, Mr. Winter. On the contrary. Mr. Silva reported you have good classroom values, and that although your teaching manner is cold, you appear to care for the students."

"Mr. Silva told me the reason he was leaving the class was that his wife was ill."

"He merely wished to explain his absence."

"With cancer. It caused me considerable distress." As he said this he noticed that Mr. Peters was holding his hand in front of his face, as though to block his eyes from the glare of sun. But they were indoors, and sky outside was grey and getting greyer.

"Is something wrong?" Winter now asked.

"Ah! You noticed! A terrible habit. Sometimes when I am interviewing people I like to look first at the top half, then the bottom half of their faces. If you've never tried this you'd be surprised how different these two halves of people's faces can be. Actually it's an excellent exercise for your class. A real attention-getter. Go ahead, try it on me."

Winter held his hand out. The top half of Peter's face featured eyes and eyebrows. He looked as though he might be posing as a candidate for a glasses commercial.

"Well?"

"The top half of your face is very. . ." Winter searched for the correct word, "photogenic. Also horizontal."

"Photogenic I like. But horizontal?"

Winter realized it was time to say the right thing. "Horizontal. Well, perhaps it's an effect of having a large forehead. Big brain capacity."

"When I had my head analyzed," Peters said, "I was told the top half was wise and just, the bottom predatory and cunning. I liked that, the split between the hunter and the judge, the active and the passive." He held his hand up and looked at Winter. "To tell the truth I see a different type of configuration in your case. The top half has a strange resemblance to a carrot, the bottom to a rabbit."

"That's good," Winter said, "perhaps I *will* have my students try it."

"But we were talking about. . ."

"Mr. Silva. The fact that he told me his wife had cancer. I think, on reflection, that was an unfriendly thing to do."

"Perhaps he went too far. But our agents, to succeed, must have a flair for the dramatic, Mr. Winter. Their task is to get into the skin, as we say, of the students, to try to see you, the teachers, from their point of view. As I told you, you came out very well. The only complaint he had, and this is a minor one, is that your knowledge of contemporary literature seemed surprisingly weak. He said you confused Margaret Laurence and D.H. Lawrence."

"Ah."

"I've never heard of either of them myself. Perhaps he was trying to be clever."

"And the teacher who complained? Should I start giving marks for life experience?"

"I don't think so. In fact, Mr. Winter, with Mr. Silva's good report in hand, I advised her to take advantage of your long experience in the classroom and get to know you a bit better. As I said to her, 'When we are young, we can find much to admire in one who has survived.'"

For their first dinner together, Winter had been intending to make lasagna for Doreen. They had tried it once in their Mum and Dad days; it had turned out disastrously, several layers of curded cheese and dried-out noodles so inedible that one of Doreen's friends had immortalized the occasion by sticking in a few birthday candles and taking a picture.

But by the time Winter left the Board of Education, it was after four o'clock. He decided on something easier and more reliable, a roast. He stopped at the butcher's and the liquor store on the way home; when he got to his apartment he popped the roast along with some onions, carrots and potatoes in the oven. Then he opened the first bottle of wine and began to drink.

The next evening he met Vivian Keller in the theatre lobby, as planned. It wasn't snowing, but walking to the theatre Winter had found the air bracingly cold, and he couldn't help congratulating himself for having had the courage to carry out this last act of the farce.

Vivian was dressed in cleavage and perfume. Sitting beside her as the play unrolled—a terrifying re-creation of torture under a military dictatorship—Winter felt not unpleasantly enveloped in Vivian's scent and warmth. So what if she had tried to get him fired? In the end he'd be dead anyway. Meanwhile he could enjoy Vivian and consider the art of revenge.

At intermission he got them drinks. White wine for Vivian, a double Scotch for himself.

"I have something terrible to confess," Vivian said, leaning terribly close.

"Let me guess."

"This is serious."

"The top of my head looks like a carrot, the bottom like a rabbit."

Vivian broke out laughing, spraying them both with white wine. She wiped her throat with her handkerchief, then dabbed at Winter's mouth. It was as though they were a married couple; Winter couldn't help thinking he was having a sudden epidemic of playing house.

"I called the Board of Education to get your phone number," she said, "and I ended up speaking to a most peculiar gentleman. Before I knew it, he'd made me tell him you don't give enough credit for 'life experience.'"

"I don't have any life experience," Winter said. "I just hover." The bell had begun to ring for the spectators to take their seats.

"I hope I didn't get you into trouble."

"Am I supposed to believe this?"

Vivian took his arm and led him back to their seat. During the whole second act she held onto his hand, as though it was something she'd long ago lost, and now wanted to make sure never to lose again.

When Winter got home it was very late. Or perhaps

early. He took his shoes off at the door. All the lights in the apartment were out, Doreen's door was closed. It was strange to be trying to undress silently in his own apartment. But he did. And, as he had every night since Doreen's arrival, he took care to put on the blue ship-patterned pyjamas he'd bought the same day he found her pink chenille bedspread. When he closed his eyes he felt he was still wrapped in Vivian Keller's scent. At her apartment after the play he had ended up telling her one of the most boring of his theories, that memory wasn't just stored in the brain but encoded in the bones. Vivian had said that, coincidentally, she believed the same thing. Also that people repeated in their current lives events from their past ones: for example, she was sure they had gone to a play, or at least a concert in a previous life and then she had said she had even dreamed that concert, it was Mozart's Twenty-first Piano Concerto and she asked him if he would mind if she turned the lights down, put on the concerto, and they would both try to remember being there. Winter stretched out on the carpet, as she suggested, and the concerto started. "This will help your bones remember," she whispered. She began massaging him. At one point her lips closed over his collarbone and he had remembered, weirdly, the previous life in which Fenny did the exact same thing, except that where Fenny's lips had been pink and springy, Vivian's were dark and lush, soaked in all that life experience for which one life might not be enough.

When he woke up the next morning, Saturday morning, it was already ten o'clock. He poked his head out of his bedroom. The apartment was silent, there was no smell of breakfast. Doreen's door was still closed. He tiptoed to the bathroom and took a shower. When he was finished he dressed, went to the kitchen and noisily began making a Spanish omelette, the kind Doreen used to like, along with a pot of strong coffee.

When everything was ready he called her name, then popped in some toast. He went to her bedroom door and called her name again. When there was no response he knocked. Knocked louder. Finally he opened the door.

The room was as it had been two mornings before. The bedspread tightly drawn, every article in the room at strict and ordered attention. The only difference was that the green suitcase and the toilet articles were missing. Even the book on UFOs was gone. There was no note. Nothing to indicate she hadn't simply been sucked into outer space for one of those examinations people always tell magazines they've been subjected to. Winter tried to imagine Doreen laid out on the operating table. She would be covered in armour, her features set and rigid. The top half of her face would be saying, "Do this to me and I will do something very awful back to you." The bottom half would have the same message. They would let her go, as quickly as possible.

The next week he received a letter.

Dear Bernard,

At the library on Friday I received a call that my husband had suffered a heart attack. I rushed back to the apartment to pack, then was in such a panic to get to the airport that I forgot to leave a note. You know how I hate the telephone, so I hope you will forgive the time it has taken you to receive this letter.

I had meant, before I was called away, to tell you about my husband, a wonderful man. I wanted to express the hope you would somehow emerge from the overlong mourning period you've been in since I refused to marry you, and find comparable happiness in your own life.

Bernard, he has the same name as you which although strange, I don't mind, it makes me feel somehow reconciled, has already completely recovered. It was some kind of false alarm. Trust a doctor to marry a hypochondriac.

It was wonderful to see you again after all these years. I cannot thank you enough for your kindness and hospitality. I hope we shall see each other again soon, and of course you must know now that you would be the most welcome of guests at our house. In the meantime my apologies and my very best wishes,

Doreen

darwin's jars

AARON FINE HAS gone up to his parents' cottage to ready it for winter. In front of the picture window is a prow-shaped deck with benches built inside the rail and, in the summer, a barbecue in the centre. Aaron has covered the barbecue with a black vinyl hood, rolled it into its sheltered all-season corner, and is now looking down at the lake and thinking that his parents, in their old age, have passed him this task at the very moment he feels himself being threatened by time. Out of nowhere it has appeared and surrounded him like a crust, an ever-thickening brittle shell beneath which the rest of him will grow soft and gooey. Meanwhile, the soft and gooey inner self is savouring the breeze, eating a ham and mustard sandwich, and wondering how cold the water will feel when he wades out to free the sand filter and the plastic pipe that feed the pump beneath the cottage.

Aaron, it should be said, is a film-maker who between bouts of compulsive reading and nervous collapse almost earns a respectable living writing for television. When unemployed he has the habit of imagining himself in the midst of a movie that is being shown to an audience whose reactions he also supplies.

At this moment on his father's deck, Aaron is picturing the silhouetted heads of his audience peering forward in the darkened theatre. What's this story going to be? they will be wondering. An arty requiem for summer? Or one of those bizarre hard-edged mystery-thrillers about a city guy getting terrorized by a strange rural cult or a resentful farmer who's beginning to suspect his so-called way of life is just a boring speck of dust trapped between the pages of a history book?

Meanwhile the camera has decided to celebrate the slanty light of the fall sun on the water. As the frame enlarges to include the shore, we suddenly notice the figure that's been there all along: a small boy wearing rolled-up jeans and a striped T-shirt. He has been watching Aaron the whole time Aaron was gazing out at what he thought was landscape.

"Have you seen my dog?" the boy asks Aaron. He's about four years old and Aaron wonders where he came from and why he's not in school. At the same time Aaron is remembering some sounds he heard in the dark late last night. A coyote, he had thought. Or a porcupine or escaped prisoners crawling through the underbrush. Of course the audience isn't aware of this. They just see the boy with his jeans rolled up higher on one side than the other, showing a strip of ankle above his running shoes.

"His name is Daisy," he adds. His cheeks are pinkly cherubic and his mouth is open, showing very white and slightly splayed milk teeth. Aaron—and the audience—can see this child is the picture of absolute hope and innocence, everything Aaron has lost. As though to emphasize the lesson the kid takes a fistful of dirt out of his pocket, opens it to extract a worm which he sets on the ground where it wriggles into the grass and disappears.

"My foot hurts," the boy says. Aaron looks down at the boy's running shoes. They are scuffed and caked with mud. The boy lifts up one foot, as though to step forward, loses his balance and begins to fall. Aaron catches him under the arms, swings him up to sit on the deck. The boy's skin is hot through his shirt, and he puts his hands trustingly on Aaron's arms as though his entire intention had been to give himself over to the care of this stranger.

"Which one?"

"There," the boy points.

Aaron loosens the laces of the shoe and then, as the shoe comes off, sees that the boy's sock is soaked in blood. Without even thinking about all the diseases that will later make a slow parade through his mind, he strips off the sock and as he lifts the foot spots the small chunk of glass that has embedded itself in the sole of the boy's foot, just where the heel ends, the skin grows softer and the arch begins. He picks the boy up again, this time cradling him in his arms, and carries him into the cottage. Again he is amazed by the warm trust of this young body and even more by the fierceness of his own paternal response.

"Will you tell me your name?" Aaron asks.

"Yes," the boy says. There is a silence. Aaron has the boy sitting on the kitchen counter beside the sink and is running water to wash the boy's foot, which is still dripping blood onto the floor. Aaron raises it to slow the bleeding.

"What *is* your name?"

"Paul."

"Paul. That's a nice name. Let me shake your foot, Paul. My name is Aaron."

"Mr. Fine."

"That's right. Aaron Fine. How did you know?"

"My father's always saying not to walk on Mr. Fine's beach."

As he dabs Paul's foot with paper towels Aaron imagines his father, the real Mr. Fine, having some sort of run-in with Paul's father. He remembers being Paul's age or a bit older and marvelling at the way his father's face would turn sour and hostile at every encounter with a stranger.

As he fixes Paul's foot, Aaron explains what he is doing. Paul watches, never flinching except when Aaron applies disinfectant, which makes his face screw up and tears jump from the corners of his eyes.

Even after he gets the bandage on, Paul's cut is still leaking blood and Aaron begins to think he should be taken to a doctor or a hospital. He finds a clean sock and slides it carefully over Paul's toes and the bandage. The sock is so large he has to roll it at the ankle.

"Where do you live, Paul?"

The boy looks around the room, then points towards the lake. "Over there."

Aaron puts Paul's bloody sock and his shoe into a plastic bag. Then he carries Paul outside. From the deck can be seen a few of the neighbouring cottages. Aaron knows none of those could belong to Paul's family.

"If I drive you home, do you know which way to go?"

Paul shakes his head. For the first time he looks a bit nervous. He sucks his lips in.

"Did you walk here on the road?"

Paul shakes his head again.

"Along the beach?"

"Through there."

Paul points towards the cottages. Aaron lifts Paul to his shoulders. Paul wraps his legs around Aaron's neck and puts a hand on Aaron's head.

"Okay, Paul, I'll be the horse. You point the way you came. I'll carry you home like this. Okay?"

Aaron starts walking towards the place he first saw Paul. Miraculously, when he gets there, Paul raises his arm, points and directs: "Through those trees."

Aaron carries Paul across the rocky terrain just back of the lake along what he gradually sees is a path that leads past all the cottages to a house visible neither from the lake nor the cottage road, a small white frame house in the midst of a scrubby meadow of hay, thistles and thorny bushes, a field centred by the house and an old paintless barn, a field in which, as he crosses it, he sees that little holes have been dug, apparently at random, perhaps by some vole or mole or groundhog type of animal or even by a human being since each hole has what appears to be a little pile of spaded-up dirt beside it.

As he approaches the barn Aaron sees that a man is standing in the shadowed open doorway, watching them. The September breeze is cool, but he is wearing shorts and sandals, and his plaid shirt is unbuttoned. His stumpy legs are tanned, and as he narrows his eyes on Paul one of his hands strokes his belly, will keep stroking it, in fact, during Aaron's whole explanation of how it happens that he has appeared with Paul on his shoulders, the child's shoe and sock in a plastic bag tied to his belt and his bandaged foot dangling on Aaron's shirt which is now spotted with blood.

"Name's Gerrard," the man says. "Walton Gerrard. My friends call me Walt, as in 'Walt, who goes there.'" He pronounces all this without a twitch of a smile, as though unaware of the incongruity of his appearance and slow drawl on the one hand, and the actual words he is saying on the other.

"Aaron Fine," Aaron says. "One of those cottages up the shore."

"Used to check your father's roof for snow in the winters."

Now Aaron knows what must have happened. After his first stroke, his father forgot how to write his name. The second stroke took away his arithmetic. One of his jobs had been the household bills and by the time his mother discovered what was happening, a lot of cheques had gone unwritten, apparently including the one to Walton Gerrard, aka Walt as in Walt payment.

"I think Paul should see someone about his foot."

Walt Gerrard holds out his arms. Aaron lifts Paul from his shoulders and passes him over. As Paul settles into his father's arms, Aaron starts to back away.

"Might as well show you what I got inside," Walt says. He is holding the boy's injured foot in one broad hand, but seems otherwise unconcerned as he steps into the barn's interior. Aaron follows through a passageway between two sets of unoccupied horse stalls which give on to a huge work area. In its midst, half reconstructed, is what Aaron thinks he recognizes as a post-war Ford, a 1953 classic with the cylindrical taillights that, as the fifties went on, gave way to the giant finned dinosaurs that ruled the continent's highways during his childhood, dinosaurs that might have reigned forever had not the asteroid of cheap foreign cars smashed into the heart of Detroit consumer loyalty and begun the Western World's precipitous decline into barbarism, etc.

Of course only the members of the Fairleigh Motoroma Club, mostly, like himself, children of car dealers, understand the exact origins of this historic sea change—yet evidence of it is everywhere to be found, Walt Gerrard's unconscious attempt to re-create civilization by rebuilding a 1953 Ford in his falling-down barn being an example. It occurs to Aaron that he could do a science fiction film about all the different people in every corner of the continent who like Walt are attempting to put civilization back on its feet by restoring old cars.

"Must be hard to get the parts," Aaron says.

"The worst was the radio. Some places you could pay five hundred dollars."

Large areas of the old Ford are swathed in masking tape, and the exposed sweeps of metal are painted with red undercoating except for the trunk. It has been painted a gleaming yellowish cream that might have been the perfect match for the cream given by the cows that lived in this barn back when this car was new for the first time, not some unconscious blood-coloured Frankenstein re-creation rising out of bandages and spare parts.

Bandages remind Aaron of Paul's foot. The boy is down on the floor now, gingerly limping about, and in one corner Aaron sees a broom angled over a small pile of shattered glass.

"His sock was too bloody to put back on," Aaron says. "I gave him one of mine. I think his foot is still bleeding."

Walt looks at Aaron, his big face blank or perhaps aggressive, Aaron couldn't say which. "The wife comes home at noon with the car."

To go the doctor's office, Walt puts on an old blue melton windbreaker with "University of Texas" stitched in yellow letters across the back. In the waiting room he unzips the jacket but buttons up his shirt. Aaron sits beside him because, having driven him—"the wife" hasn't appeared and the pre-dinosaur Ford is an engine job away from hitting the road again—he isn't going to wait outside in the parking lot.

Paul is on Walt's lap, leafing through a comic. He still has a shoe on one foot, a bandage and Aaron's sock—now brown with dried blood—on the other. Aaron is still carrying the matching shoe and bloody sock in a plastic bag, as though he might be required to show it in order to justify the whole absurd situation. After the doctor checks out Paul's foot will come the time for putting a proper shoe and sock on it. But Aaron hasn't wanted to say anything about this; he's afraid Walt will view it as an intrusion. Aaron decides that while waiting for the doctor, he will slip out to the supermarket on the pretext of buying a paper, and pick up a pair of boys' running shoes which he'll say he just happened to have in his car for his nephew.

His errand accomplished, Aaron is in the supermarket parking lot telephone booth dialling the telephone number of his own apartment. Soon he will be speaking to Rose. Coincidentally, his late grandmother was also called Rose. A few weeks ago Aaron gave the living Rose, for her thirty-second birthday, a picture of his grandmother Rose at the same age. With her flapper hair and demure lips-compressed smile she bore a distinct resemblance to the woman with whom her grandson now shared his life.

"I hate the way you say we share our lives," Rose once said. "I know you mean to be funny but it makes our relationship sound like a big waterbed we sloosh around on."

Aaron hated the way Rose had said "our relationship." It sounded like a dark cupboard to which only she had the key.

His plan is to tell Rose he has been caught up in a strange drama that started with an unknown neighbour boy looking for his dog, and that therefore he will be staying at the cottage overnight. When she answers the phone he hears music he doesn't recognize in the background and the sound of two glasses clinking together.

"Having some sort of party?" Aaron asks without preliminary.

"Not exactly."

Aaron hopes Rose is wearing something.

"I won't be back tonight," Aaron says.

"Okay," says Rose.

When he gets back to the doctor's office, Aaron is so upset by what he heard over the phone that he carries the shoes into the waiting room.

"Gerrards," the nurse calls out. The door to the doctor's office opens and Aaron sees the doctor himself, Henry Vernon. Aaron has driven in with his mother a couple of times when she needed something for her diabetes. Dr. Vernon had always looked at him somewhat malignantly, Aaron thinks, as if to say that sooner or later his time will come.

Walt stands up and starts to carry Paul towards the office. His legs are strongly bowed, and as he walks his sandals slap between the floor and the soles of his feet. At the nurse's desk he stops and looks around to Paul. "If the wife comes in, you can tell her where we are."

The entrance of "the wife" is crucial to the story. One of those doors through which a story walks and is changed forever.

Would Walt's wife be a creature physically like Walt himself, for example, a large blonde woman wearing overalls? Or will she match the car he is reconstructing and be a dark-haired Barbara Stanwyck type wearing a pleated skirt and a trench coat?

The wife turns out to be young, mid-twenties at most, and featuring a classic combination of long red-auburn hair and turquoise eyes that, as Aaron would later explain to Rose, "literally shone like jewels."

Aaron's immediate thought is how unfair it is Walt has this incredibly beautiful woman while he himself, the humble saint who rescued Walt's son from bleeding to death in his shoe, is locked in a dark cupboard of a relationship with a woman who appears to be screwing a stranger. And yet even during the fraction of a second it takes Aaron to register all these related injustices, he also realizes this extraordinary woman is not only the source of Walt's eerie rock-like confidence but doubtless enjoys leaning on it, whereas he, Aaron, could provide nothing to lean on but endlessly recycled doubt.

"You must be Paul's mother," Aaron says.

The woman is carrying a large bag. From the bag she withdraws a new pair of boy's running shoes and white socks joined together by a plastic clip that she removes before smoothing the socks with her thumbs.

At a certain point after his eventual return to Toronto, Aaron tries to make neutral conversation out of his theory that foreign cars are destroying civilization by sending America into a crisis of self-doubt it can resolve only by violent movies and sex-crazed politicians.

"Deep down, that stuff is what you really believe," Rose says.

Her voice is, all things considered, complaisant. I do believe it, Aaron thinks of saying. But the horrible truth is that not only Western civilization but his own heart has been eaten away from the inside. For example, he hardly has the moral strength to object to her being unfaithful while he was up at the cottage saving the water line from freezing and the neighbour's boy from bleeding to death.

"If you were Penelope and I were Odysseus, think what I might have done," Aaron says.

"Penelope had suitors."

"She didn't invite them up for drinks."

"She fed them all the time. Herds of sheep. Fields of artichokes. Seas of lobster and crab. Along with whole villages of servant girls who were ravished in order that Penelope be spared."

"She never allowed anyone in her bedroom."

"Either you trust me or you don't."

Aaron is in the bathtub. After everything that happened at his parents' cottage a bath is what he needs, but because he is still fighting with Rose he has decided to protect his modesty by using bubble bath. Only his feet, which are very long, and his head, which has suffered a loss of dignity because of a few clusters of bubbles sticking to his hair, are visible.

Rose is sitting on the toilet seat. She is saying, "I can't

believe, after what you've accused me of, that you are now telling me you've met the love of your life."

"You should see her eyes."

"What did you do with her?"

"Aren't you jealous?"

"I'm curious."

"I said, 'Look, why don't we leave the running shoes on our chairs and go for a drive.'"

"Perfect."

"All right, I didn't do anything. We just sat speechlessly staring into each other's eyes and after a while she said, 'Aaron, if we still feel this way in a week, let's meet at the place written on this piece of paper that I'm holding in my mouth and am going to put in your mouth without using my hands.'"

"For God sakes, Aaron, I have an old boyfriend over for an innocent drink and you're so jealous of him that you have to make up bad movies? I thought we were going to share our lives, not our mental illnesses."

"I hate the way it sounds when you say 'share our lives.'"

"So do I."

When Walt and Paul emerge from the examining room, Paul begins to wriggle in Walt's arms as soon as he sees his mother. She takes him on her lap, examines the bandage the doctor has applied, slides a new sock and shoe onto the injured foot, then changes the good one.

"It was really nice of you to help out," she says to Aaron. She rises, holding Paul, and leans into Walt. The three of them stand for a moment, so absolutely still they could be a massive rock sculpture. A massive rock sculpture so heavy that the entire waiting room and everyone in it is revolving around them. The silence isn't broken: the moment lasts forever until, from somewhere deep inside the perfect unmoving iconic triangle, a lock gives way and Walt's arm begins to turn the wife towards the door at the same time as the wife herself begins to move and Paul raises his hand to wave goodbye to Aaron.

Aaron is at his parents' cottage. An outside light shows snow falling outside. Aaron has a fire going in the wood stove and is standing on a stepladder, completing the task of insulating the cottage walls. The wind gusts and there is a sound that might be snow battering the walls. Or is it someone at the door? Aaron pauses to listen. The audience wonders if this is the big moment, when Walt will appear, or Paul, or even the woman with the turquoise eyes. We are also aware that the title needs to be resolved.

Darwin's Jars, everyone is thinking. This kind of movie attracts an audience that already knows—or has read in some pompous review—that Darwin's theory of evolution had something to do with the fact that every acre of British soil contains 170,000 earthworms. Did Darwin actually count them? Who can say? We only remember that these worms worked hard, eating and breeding; and that as Newton saw the apple fall, Darwin observed the progress of his worms.

Some viewers might also remember that Darwin was once a biologist on an ocean voyage. He survived a few storms, saw many faraway flora and fauna, and—here's the crucial bit of information—collected specimens in jars!

Now that we're getting towards the end of the movie, the audience remembers the worm in Paul's pocket. And the random holes dug in the field. Instead of a car in that barn, there should have been a scientific laboratory. Walt should have been a nutty biologist instead of a nut with a working wife and a forty-five-year-old car he was planning to drive in a parade in two years if he could get the right radio.

Aaron goes to the door and opens it. There's a swirl of snow, nothing else. He closes the door and walks towards the stove. The camera follows him, then stops at a framed picture of his grandmother. Everyone was once someone else, we think. Deep down we're glad this isn't a story about worms. It is a story about Aaron's grandmother's grandson.

Evolution! the audience suddenly realizes, is an ironic concept in this movie. Aaron hasn't evolved at all! Before emigrating to Canada, his grandmother lived in some mythic frozen shtetl in the mythic frozen tundra, huddled with her family around a stove with just a few faggots of wood to keep them warm until they got killed in a pogrom. And now here is Aaron, generations down the line but no better off. Somehow he has thrown away his refined girl-friend, his university education and all the advantages his parents struggled to give him, and is out in the middle of nowhere trying to keep warm. *Darwin's Jars!* Must be some brand of home-made vodka that peasants' grandchildren drink to keep themselves ignorant.

The audience now understands that Aaron has deluded himself into thinking he is living a big adventure. Rejecting the constraints of city life and the insincere subtleties of modern urban relationships, Aaron believes he has decided to make another choice.

In his fantasies he has bought a black half-ton truck, wears a sheepskin jacket, and has taken to smoking ciga-rettes he rolls himself. But the reality is that after leaving his and Rose's apartment he went to his parents' place to dump his six cartons of possessions in the basement, and while rooting around in what was once the canning room discovered his old sleeping bag and the pair of cross-country skis he bought to impress a certain long-gone Amanda.

The noise of the storm recedes and the scene ends with Aaron staring pensively at the insulation.

Early the next morning Aaron is woken by a fierce knocking at his door. In the background a huge motor is revving, and his first thought is that he has been tracked down by helicopter police. He rolls out of his sleeping bag on the couch, fully dressed except for his shoes, and stumbles to the door. Brilliant sunshine penetrates the sheet he hung over the picture window. When he opens the door he sees it's the wife, in full Technicolor enhanced by a crazy little mauve toque.

"Hey," she says. "I didn't mean to wake you up."

On his lawn is an idling snowmobile, straddled by Walt who gives him a big wave and calls out, "Georgia wants to invite you to dinner."

That night Aaron straps on his cross-country skis and, following the trail Walt has so thoughtfully provided, "The white carpet treatment," as Walt says, makes his way through moonlit pines and poplars to the white frame farmhouse for dinner. The temperature has fallen but the thin quarter moon is enough to set the entire countryside aglow and decorate his path with long spindly shadows. In case he gets lost on this journey, Aaron has put a few emergency supplies in his knapsack: a plastic space tent that comes folded up in a wallet-sized package, a box of wooden matches along with several candles to provide light and to heat the tent, four nutritionally guaranteed multi-grain bars, a small pot with a collapsible handle, and of course a Swiss army knife for cutting firewood and slaughtering small animals. He also has a bottle of wine, which he offers to Walt at the door. Walt smiles and says, "Nice of you to bring it but I meant to tell you that I make my own."

Like his car, Walt's house is a work of art still being worked on. In the centre of the main floor—a large recently opened space where outlines of the walls that used to be can still be seen—is a beautiful glass-doored wood stove glowing with heat. The living-dining area has plywood flooring decorated by Paul's crayon drawings, jotted construction calculations, spills from previous celebratory evenings. But the kitchen area has large blue ceramic tiles and the cabinetry and appliances are grouped in a dark polished U.

Walt is wearing grease-stained jeans, his trademark unbuttoned plaid shirt and a T-shirt that ripples as he rubs his belly. Georgia has tight grey Spandex slacks and a fuzzy green sweater on top with a V-neck that reveals a pearl necklace glowing against her flushed throat.

On the far side of the room is a new staircase rising to the second floor. The steps, the banister rail, along with the railings themselves, are of a flaming maple that catches the light from the glass-doored stove. Walt must have made them, Aaron realizes. As with his antique car, every detail has been carefully attended to. If it took him a month instead of a week—or for that matter twenty years—Aaron now knows Walt would have kept doing and redoing every joint until the staircase in its solid geometric perfection rose like a ladder to heaven from his newly renovated living room to the bedrooms above. Aaron wonders if Walt makes love the same way, working every cell of the wife's body until she lights up in the darkness, an illuminated cathedral on whose altar he performs the ritual sacrament of the flesh.

His coat taken and his boots removed, Aaron moves towards the kitchen. Paul is watching cartoons on television. As Aaron passes he raises a foot and wiggles his toes in greeting. Beside his armchair is a gracefully curled Dalmatian. "Daisy?" Aaron asks. Paul wiggles his toes again.

Walt's home-made wine comes complete with a beige label with a string of grapes on top and, handwritten beneath: *Walt and Georgia, 1998.* "It's a mixture of grapes and dandelions," Walt explains. "Georgia got the idea from a magazine."

Georgia smiles. She possesses, Aaron now sees, a spectacular smile. Something about the way her upper lip is slightly smaller than her lower lip, making her smile as much a V as a curve. "I'm a television director," Aaron considers announcing. "I'd love to cast you in my next film." At this exact moment he has no next film, and when he does everything will happen so fast he won't have time to audition the neighbour down the road. On the other hand he could write something specially for her. As he watches Walt twist out the cork, he imagines the camera moving in close to Georgia's face.

"I know this sounds stupid," Georgia is saying, her classic turquoise eyes brimming with tears, "but I married him because he got me pregnant on a date-rape drug. I guess that's what happens when you're a Catholic." The camera moves back and we see she is sitting at a candlelit restaurant table.

Aaron is leaning towards her sympathetically and he says, "That's terrible. What a brute. Someone should teach him a lesson."

Georgia gasps and reaches to clutch Aaron's hand. "No! You don't know him. He's—"

It is after dinner at Walt and Georgia's. The electric lights have been turned off and the room is filled with a golden glow provided by several strategically placed kerosene lamps. Three beige-labelled bottles are clustered together in the centre of the dining table. "That was fabulous," Aaron says. He attempts to move his arm, which is either paralyzed or disconnected, towards his glass of water. A twelve-lane headache is roaring through his skull. Walt is sitting across from him. Georgia has taken Paul up to bed.

"I used to use a few aspirins before drinking this stuff," Walt says, "but one night they made my stomach bleed."

Aaron and Georgia are in a convertible, top down, driving along a road at the edge of the Pacific. Georgia is wearing a white silk scarf that streams in the moonlight. She turns to Aaron and puts her hand on his arm. "Somehow I know I can trust you," she says. "I *can* count on you, can't I?"

Aaron smiles weakly. "Sure," he says. He and the audience realize the obvious: the whole time Aaron thought he was rescuing first Paul and then Georgia, Georgia has been setting him up to kill Walt. Her plan is to live on the insurance money while Aaron rots in jail.

"It's for the boy's sake," Georgia says.

"I know," Aaron murmurs.

He stops the car at a large cliff.

"What are you doing?" Georgia asks.

"My father always told me it was good luck to look over a cliff at midnight. Reminds you how great it is to be alive."

"That's so poetic," Georgia says.

Aaron gets out of the car, comes round and opens her door.

"My father *was* a poet," Aaron says as they walk towards the moon, the sea, the abyss.

The audience senses a subtle shift in the balance of power. They are standing on the edge. Aaron is saying something about his father's poetry but the crashing waves are louder than his words and all we can make out is something about his father killing himself.

"Why?" Georgia asks.

"My mother pushed him to it."

Aaron has his hand on Georgia's back and we know she is as good as gone. In a brilliant cinematic moment for which he will always be remembered, Aaron is going to save himself from the manipulative Georgia, take revenge on his anti-poetic mother, and bring his Cannes Palme d'Or feature to its startling and unexpected climax.

Aaron and Walt are in Walt's barn. Aaron is huddled into his ski jacket. Walt has his own jacket open and is comfortably scratching his belly. They are standing beside Walt's 1953 Ford renovation project. It is now virtually complete, a gleaming cream-and-maroon masterpiece with a working radio that is broadcasting a hockey game. The aerial has a raccoon tail, and as they talk Walt gives the hood ornament a few swipes. In his other hand he has a newly opened bottle of "Walt and Georgia, '98."

"It's looking great," Aaron says. "Soon you're going to need a new project."

"Already have one. Want to see it?"

"Sure."

Walt straightens up and walks to a door Aaron hadn't noticed, pushes it open.

"This way," Walt says.

Aaron follows Walt into the darkness.

"Used to be the stalls back here," Walt says. The only light is from the half-open door behind them. "Yeah, here we go. Just around this corner."

Now there's no light at all. Suddenly there's a loud grunt from Aaron, the sound of him falling.

Aaron is kneeling on the floor, clutching his stomach.

"Gotta watch the corner of that table," Walt says. "Sorry, I should have warned you." There's the click of a switch and Aaron sees they are in some weird kind of storage room. Tables line the walls, and above them, freshly and carefully constructed in Walt's meticulous way, shelves rise to the high ceiling. On the shelves and tables are a huge variety of jars and glass containers. Each holds fragments of bones or, sometimes, completely reconstructed skeletons.

"Look at this," Walt says. It seems to be a groundhog and it's in a large bell jar with a narrow neck. "Getting these things in here is like building a ship in a bottle. You wouldn't believe how long it takes." He peers at Aaron. "Hey, you know these things are fake, don't you? They come in halves and you just glue them together at the end."

He flicks another switch and across the room two long fluorescent lights begin to wink and glow. The lights are suspended above a long table and on the table is a large glass coffin with what looks to be a human skeleton.

"This is my best one," Walt says.

Every bone has been meticulously cleaned and varnished. Walt must have taken the whole thing apart, worked on it for weeks or months, then put it back together, just like his reconditioned car.

"I'd say it's about perfect except for the left foot and ankle. You wonder if something ate it away or maybe even the family kept it for a souvenir. What do you think?"

Aaron keeps moving away from Walt so that Walt won't ever be between him and the door.

"I figure it's the guy who settled the place. There was a dog cemetery out back, then I found this little cross about a hundred feet off. Must have been painted white, probably had some words, but everything was worn away."

"What made you dig it up?" Aaron asks, wondering who Walt killed and how he can think anyone will ever believe his story. Or maybe Aaron isn't intended to believe it. Maybe this is just the line Walt feeds his victims before he begins to do whatever he does to them.

"Saw the way the cross was rotting and, well—" Walt stops and reaches into his shirt to scratch his belly, "—it didn't seem right that some fellow would be down there in an old falling-apart pine box, his clothes all a mess, when I could clean him up, give him a proper resting place."

"Couldn't have been easy."

"Nope. Those bones were covered in all sorts of crap. Had to use this—" Walt picks up a large hook-bladed knife, and that's when Aaron runs.

Aaron arrives at what used to be the apartment and the life he shared with Rose at six in the morning. Streaming sweat he runs up the stairs and pounds on the door, not wanting to use his key in case Rose is in bed with one of her boyfriends. When she answers, comfortingly wrapped in a flannelette nightgown and housecoat, they throw their arms around each other and she murmurs something about never letting him go again. They make love wildly during which Aaron does his best not to see the varnished skeleton in its glass coffin.

The next morning Rose convinces Aaron that by going to the police he will only make a fool of himself.

"Look," Rose says, "even if it is illegal to dig people up, you don't really want Walt to be put in jail for it. What would happen to his wife and child?" Aaron sees himself standing in a witness box, wearing prison stripes. Georgia, beautifully dressed in black, stares at him through her tear-stained veil. Paul has taken off one of his shoes and is waving it at Aaron.

"You're right," Aaron says. He and Rose go out into the sunny winter morning. The streets are jammed, cars are honking, passersby are passing, but Aaron and Rose are oblivious. Hand in hand they stroll and the camera follows them until they reach the art cinema where they first met. There the camera stops. Aaron and Rose fade into the distance as the image blurs and the closing credits begin to roll.

shelter

THE KNOCK AT THE DOOR came just after lunch. Martin Wahl was at home, standing in front of the hall mirror adjusting his tie. Also his face—from that of an anxiously unemployed male dreading his upcoming birthday to, he hoped, the reassuring face of competence, a face any employer would want on his team.

The knock was firm, polite, certainly not loud. Martin turned towards the door and saw a man backing away from the double triangles of glass.

For a moment Martin considered ignoring the stranger—but these days he was finding strangers difficult to ignore. Since losing his job he had become increasingly aware that the streets were now the property of a swelling tide of homeless panhandlers, drugged-out chemically controlled mental patients, weirdly pierced and dyed teenagers and unemployed time-killers like himself. He couldn't seem to go out the door without feeling he'd been sucked into the undertow of the hordes who had unluckily fallen from grace and now roamed the city in search of food and shelter. "Look at them," he had said to Julia, just the other night, as they drove by a group of striking postal workers warming themselves around a barrel of burning construction debris. Admiring the flames and sharing the warmth were two women with shopping carts crammed with blankets and clothes. Also someone Martin recognized: a formerly well-known book collector who had lost his job as a government social worker and currently passed his days soliciting hand-outs from his former neighbours and clients. A Czechoslo-vakian refugee, he often talked to himself as he walked, and he was said to sleep in a corner of a former friend's garage that backed onto an alleyway behind the fish-and-chip shop two blocks from Martin's house. Rumour had it that he had several times been taken to a downtown psychiatric hospital where he had voluntarily submitted to electro-shock therapy.

"What do you mean *them?*"

"It's like some kind of purgatory," Martin had said, "a gathering of the damned." And he wanted to say to Julia, but was afraid to expose himself, that sometimes he woke in the night and imagined that the whole city had been taken over by these clusters of the excluded and the victimized, huddled in shelters for the homeless or gathered in con-demned houses drinking and taking drugs. At one time, Martin would eventually remind himself, he also had gone to condemned houses to drink, sample drugs, even occa-sionally pick up a partner for a few sins of the flesh. Back then he hadn't thought of such an event as a night in purga-tory—he had called it a party.

When he opened the door the stranger stepped back farther, as though he knew Martin's fragile state and was taking care not to frighten him. He was tall, slender, with pallid skin and large, intense eyes. He was wearing jeans, a dark paisley shirt open at the neck to reveal a silver chain and cat's-eye pendant, and a worn leather jacket. Slung from one shoulder was a large camera case.

"Sorry," Martin said. "You'd be for the Fletchers. They moved out two years ago. I don't have an address for them."

"I wasn't looking for the Fletchers."

"I don't know who was here before them," Martin said.

The stranger nodded understandingly as Martin began to close the door. "Your wife," he said. "Julia."

Martin now noticed the coarse black hair poking through the triangle of the stranger's open shirt, the heavy rings on his fingers.

"She's not here," Martin said. "She's out of town."

"I know. She's flying here on a plane from San Francisco. Scheduled to land in exactly—" the stranger looked at his wristwatch "—two hours and eighteen minutes. So, Martin, this is our chance."

"Insurance. You're selling insurance."

One evening about a week later, while Martin was in the bedroom of the house he and Julia rented, a house that had previously been occupied by a couple whose last name was Fletcher and who still received bills from several department stores, he noticed the red blinking of the answering machine light. A double blink, to be exact, indicating two messages. He pushed the button. The first was from Harvey Adams, to say that he'd reserved a table for four at Enoteca after the concert. The second began with a silence, followed by the sound of a man clearing his throat. Martin thought Harvey must have called back to change the restaurant plan; Harvey's messages often started with an indecisive blank, followed by a mutter that gradually resolved itself into a few well-organized words. Harvey was an architect, a partner in his firm; indecipherable mumbling, along with choosing the restaurant, was one of his privileges. "Julia," the voice said. Not Harvey. Martin, contemplating the something harsh, the something possessive, in the man's tone, recognized the voice of the stranger who had come to the door. Then the machine clicked off.

In the midst of the concert Martin—who had dozed off—opened his eyes and looked at the brightly lit stage, the massed curves of orchestra players in their tuxedos and black dresses, the vigorously shaking black leonine coiffure of Amistrav Raj, the renowned conductor whose long outstretched arms were flapping enthusiastically, urging on the allegro movement of Beethoven's Sixth with a characteristic pleading gesture to the first violins—and Martin had the sudden uncanny feeling that for the first time that evening, or perhaps the first time in weeks or months or years, he was truly awake, truly inhabiting his body, truly seeing.

What did he see? He saw several hundred sets of shoulders, necks and heads turned expectantly towards the renowned and distinguished and famously sexy Mr. Raj, who had taken this opportunity to leave his arms outstretched, dramatically awaiting the first violins' response to his eloquent invitation. At this precise moment in the Pastoral, a tiny interval in the movement the concert program had called "Beethoven's raging storm," the silent centre leapt to the foreground, only to be filled by the unbearably sharp interplay between the conductor and the concertmaster—who finally raised his eyes to the conductor and tensed his fingers on the bow.

Martin's right hand cramped in sympathy. As a child he had played the violin. Now he could feel the top knuckle of his thumb digging into the mother-of-pearl casing that enclosed the taut horsehair which—in the futile hope of avoiding mistakes—Martin used to cover with such a thick film of rosin that the crown of his violin was always spotted with amber dust. He could remember the sweat pooling in his armpits, his violin teacher looking at him as though he were an unwanted insect, a subhuman barbarian insect about to sully the perfect incense-laden air of his studio with a jagged dissonant buzz. At such moments his violin teacher's mouth would curve maliciously, and he seemed on the edge of bending to give Martin an unspeakably evil kiss.

Martin could see the concertmaster's lips trembling, as though he too were desperate to avoid this evil kiss. Then, with a silken flourish, the concertmaster's arm descended and the "raging storm" parted to allow the "chorus of angels" to fill the concert hall.

Martin heard Julia sigh. My wife, he thought, *my wife*. Her lips were pursed, her cheeks hollow, her large eyes glowing. It was over three years since he had met Julia, and as he had gradually made his way into her aura, her warmth, and eventually her arms, he'd been continually amazed at the spectacle of his own unexpected and undeserved luck.

To reassure himself his luck still held, he took her hand. Her hand squeezed back and she snuggled closer to him. *My wife*, he said to himself: like his black dress pants, his patent-leather shoes, the seldom-worn but very elegant gold cuff links that his father had surprised him with on his thirtieth birthday, his silk socks with their built-in garters clinging to his calves, she was *his*. Though of course he had not married Julia to own her. He had married her, as he'd explained to Harvey—this explanation had come to him after they'd gotten as drunk as they possibly could the night before the

wedding—because Julia was like a perfect bottle of brandy
and by marrying her he was making sure the bottle would
never be empty.

"That's an amazing idea," Harvey had responded sounding less than amazed.

Harvey was sitting on Julia's other side, her non-Martin
side, and on Harvey's non-Julia side was his own wife,
Annette, a large bird-like creature who specialized in stock
options and who, after meeting Julia in a massage class, had
selected her as her protégée. Now Annette was leaning forward, apparently unaware that Harvey had fallen asleep,
and was raptly swaying with the allegro's rising crescendos.
Meanwhile Martin had the feeling that layers of pretence
were peeling away: some younger self, a young Martin
Wahl the older Martin had either forgotten or locked away
or drunk into acquiescence, had suddenly reappeared at the
controls and was looking out of the older Martin's eyes to
discover he was listening to music that bored him, wearing
clothes that itched and constrained, was holding the hand of
a woman whose fragrance came from a brand of perfume he
now remembered as belonging to a hated high-school Latin
teacher and had as his two supposed friends a couple of
middle-aged snobs whose company he always felt vaguely
ashamed for seeking.

This distaste for his older self's life lasted through the re-
mainder of the concert and once they were out of the hall,
Martin pleaded a headache to escape the late supper that had
been planned, then led Julia out into the street where with
a maestro-like wave he attracted a taxi on his first attempt.

In the middle of the night Martin woke up. He was lying on
his back, one arm flung out, the way he sometimes fell

asleep after sex. He couldn't help imagining himself in the same position, standing in front of the Toronto Philharmonic, the outflung arm calling on the concertmaster to make his contribution. On her knees, arms wrapped around his waist and head pressed imploringly to Martin's belly would be Julia. "Play it," Martin would be screaming. The concertmaster, transfixed with terror, would finally slash his bow across the strings. But instead of a comfortable melody out would leap the great loud scrawk of truth to rip away, all through the hall, the toupées and the blow-dried hair, the silk stockings, the pressed linen pants, the designer dresses and diamond brooches. All that would remain would be twelve hundred naked season-ticket-holding Torontonians, pressing their programs between their legs and wondering how to signal a taxi and preserve their modesty at the same time.

He put his hand down to stroke Julia's hair. She had fallen asleep with her lips against the thin skin that stretched over his ribs, and each time she exhaled a warm tide of breath rolled across his chest. There was something so trusting about Julia, so vulnerable. Even the first night he had entered her apartment, to receive nothing more than a chaste kiss on the cheek and a copy of the Carlos Fuentes novel she had been talking about, he had wanted to warn her that people, especially people like him, shouldn't be allowed so close to her.

When he first went out with her, he didn't try to touch her. Even the sight of her forearms, pale and perfect in the June sun, was more than he could bear. The velvety brush of her cheek. The way, when she leaned across a table, one otherwise perfect but very slightly slanted front tooth proclaimed its small imperfection with such humility that he

stared at it until, finally, utterly charmed, he had felt everyone's smile should be made perfect by such a flaw. "I can't
believe you go around that way," he'd once said.

"What way?"

Of course he couldn't explain. What way? *That* way.
Desirable. Defenceless. Sharing her air in crowded eleva-
tors. Trying on lingerie in department store changing
rooms. Sleeping with her lips open to the ribs of men she'd
married only two years ago.

He now noticed that the red light of their telephone
answering machine was winking on and off again. With
each flash a weak red glow fanned up the wall. Philip was
the name of the man who'd come to the door. "She's using
us," Philip had said. "I thought you should know. I mean, we
can't have a ménage à trois or whatever they call it without
all of us knowing. It wouldn't be fair."

Afterwards, at his job interview, Martin had found himself facing a man whose arrogance reminded him of Philip,
wearing a dark suit that hung from his shoulders in a way that
made him wonder how Philip's shoulders, apparently broad
and muscular, would appear to Julia when they were un-
clothed. When the interviewer had asked him why he was
unemployed, Martin had stumbled nervously, then explained
he had left in order to find a superior position, something in
financial management that would be a suitable prelude to
studying for an advanced degree in business administration.
"I was thinking of Harvard," Martin had concluded. The interviewer's face went flat as a cinder block while the room
filled with a large disbelieving silence—a stormy nothingness
unlikely to be interrupted by the skilful sweep of a concertmaster's bow or the sweet music of a job offer. Instead,
Martin tucked his resumé back into his briefcase and left.

After the concert and after he had very showily taken an aspirin for the imaginary headache he'd used to get out of the dinner with Harvey and Annette, Martin opened a bottle of wine and made a salad while Julia whipped up one of those perfect little omelettes she used to serve him three years ago, back when he was first worrying about her vulnerability and saying things like, "You know, there's something about these eggs, soft, warm, but not exactly puddly, that reminds me of the skin just beside your belly button," and she would pull up her sweater and stand beside him so he could test but of course the true test was lying down, that's when skin puddles if it's going to, etc., until the world had turned and they were up and in the kitchen again, this time facing omelettes with which time had had its cruel predictable way.

The next morning, when he had finished perusing the sports scores, he turned dutifully to the business section. There he found an article advising people who faced bankruptcy to "destroy" their credit cards. Martin took out his own credit card, a red-and-blue rectangle imprinted with numbers he had memorized, and placed it on the kitchen table. He imagined it being bombed by a squadron of planes piloted by steely-eyed bankers intent on keeping him from defrauding them. "It's for my own good," he imagined himself calling out as the sky filled with light and fragments of shrapnel and plastic. Then he took Julia's scissors and snipped his credit card into small triangular pieces. Bizarrely, his first wife's name was still on his credit card. *Sharon.* He took the liberty of snipping the letters of her name into especially tiny morsels. Nothing personal, in fact he remembered her with great fondness.

"What about Sharon?" Harvey had asked, the night Martin had compared Julia to a perfect bottle of brandy. "Did you spill her by mistake?"

Something like that, Martin had thought. Like his so-called career, a series of three ascending jobs in the graphic design sales business, Sharon had just drifted away. Run away, to be exact, to New Mexico with a chiropractor.

"She promoted herself," Martin liked to say, but before her self-promotion he had started having affairs with women he would meet in downtown oyster bars after his Friday afternoon squash games. Although before those oyster-bar failings Sharon had rejected him by taking up the habit of falling asleep at seven o'clock in the evening. That, Martin thought, was the problem with the past: re-seen while looking teary-eyed at a mound of plastic that once had a credit limit of eleven thousand dollars, the past was a glittering pile of jagged plastic slivers that could be re-assembled in a billion possible ways. But none of them would ever again be a credit card.

He swept the mess into a garbage can. The truth was, speaking of truth, that he wasn't the unfaithful type. Even cutting up Sharon's name with Julia's scissors made him uncomfortable. There was a thin filmy smear on the blades: he washed them off carefully with hot water and liquid detergent, then dried them with a towel.

Julia had met Martin at a party after a concert and they had gone out twice. The first date was awkward, a dinner at an Italian restaurant where they had trouble finding conversation. On the second date they went in the opposite direction—to a baseball game—and by the fifth inning had somehow been able to admit to each other that they were bored. This mutual admission made Julia think Martin might be interesting after all. She then talked about Martin to Annette, who in turn mentioned Martin to Harvey. By one of those bizarre coincidences that change lives, Harvey knew Martin from his squash club. He had even played with him once, and gave a glowing account of the younger man's agility and good manners. "You know Harvey," Annette reported to Julia, who had been taken up by the couple as a sort of third wheel, "when he says someone is a gentleman it's the ultimate compliment."

Julia didn't like Martin talking about himself as unemployed. She found it too negative. She wanted him to describe his situation as "between assignments." Or when she thought he couldn't hear her on the telephone, "Martin has decided to take a few months off to think. Isn't that wonderful?"

"Look," Martin said, "you can be with him or not, it's up to you, but I don't like him calling all the time."

They were in the kitchen eating Martin's mushroom risotto.

"I never was with him," Julia said. "We went out a few times but then——"

"Then?"

"Oh——you wouldn't understand."

"I see," Martin said. That morning, after Julia left for work, he had packed up his stereo set and taken it to a pawn shop. "It cost me two thousand dollars," Martin said. "The speakers are the best." Standing at the glass counter, Martin could remember the slightly fearful feeling he'd had when he selected them, the way he'd fingered his credit card, as though in this extravagant purchase it might betray him. "That was then," the dealer told him, "I wouldn't get a hundred for it now. I'll give you fifty." Martin had served Julia the best of the risotto, including those mushrooms that hadn't blackened and shrivelled, while he himself had a few sections of dark crust he'd scraped from the pot.

"You don't have to be jealous," Julia said, "he was a Catholic. I mean, totally hung up. I think I was about his eighteenth fiancée."

"You said you were never with him."

"We did a few things but nothing, you know, transcendent. That Catholic thing is pretty strong. Don't worry about it. We only spent one night together. Maybe two."

Martin wondered what Julia was inviting him to imagine. Possibly nothing. "Then why did he come to the door? Why does he keep telephoning?"

"I told you. He's on the twelve-step program. He has to ask everyone he might have hurt to forgive him. He wants me to forgive him for what happened between us—"

"The nothing transcendent?"

"You could put it that way."

"I see."

"And he wants you to forgive him for once having loved me. Years ago. Long before I ever met you."

Martin started arranging his rice crusts in the shape of a house. He wondered if someone would like to invest in a study of the insulating properties of stuck-together rice grains.

"Maybe I'm the one who should be asking you to forgive me," Julia said. "For existing before you. For sticking my tongue into other men's mouths. For getting them to stick their tongues into me."

Martin looked at Julia across the mound of his dried rice. In the candlelight—he had arranged for them to eat by candlelight in order to hide the extent of the disaster—her face was even more than ever its mysterious, flickering, desirable self. Of course other men had desired her. Of course she had desired other men. Had? Had he sold the last souvenir of his credit card to be told of this desire across a ruined dinner he'd spent half the afternoon preparing?

"I was thinking I might just walk out," Julia said. "Pack my suitcases and leave. Do you think I should?"

If he kept his mouth shut, Martin knew, Julia would eventually calm down. In an hour or two they would end up in bed, consoling each other. Life, *life*, non-life, would roll on, and gradually whatever they'd broken would be dissolved or encysted.

"Why don't you do whatever you want?" Martin said.

Even in the candlelight he could see the blood rushing to Julia's face. In the Toronto airport two years ago, shunted aside by customs after their honeymoon trip to Mexico, Julia had been taken to a small room and strip-searched by two female agents she later described as "two fat dykes pretending I might have a condom full of cocaine up my bum." Spitting out this very, at least in Martin's view, untypical sentence, Julia's face had turned red with fury, as it was now, and her eyes had sparked. Julia's black belt karate skills—she sometimes wore the actual belt around her waist to get in the mood before her weekend morning runs—would have enabled her to have a brief moment of glory with those customs agents; now Martin wondered if her reddening face meant she was about to leap up, smash the pine table with a thunderous chop and take revenge on him.

Instead, she began to cry.

—

"She's just playing us off against each other," Philip said. "She's making us into sex toys."

"She told me she never had anything to do with you that way. She said you wanted to ask our forgiveness."

They were in a Bloor Street coffee shop. Neutral ground that Philip had chosen for this encounter and to which Martin had agreed, thinking that nothing could be less intimate than a brightly lit restaurant full of plastic doughnuts and plastic stools. But the atmosphere was strangely convivial. A group of about a dozen striking posties were drinking coffee and loudly denouncing the government, while in another corner student couples were leaning towards each other, their shampooed hair drifting in and out of each other's orbits like intersecting haloes.

"That's why I looked her up again," Philip said. "But when we met, she told me she wanted to make up for lost time. Of course I didn't know she was married. And by the time I found out . . ."

"When you found out?"

"I guess I was always in love with her. Just a bit. Then by the time I found out, this time around, she had my heart on a string, in her pocket, I don't know, some kind of voodoo."

"Great," Martin said. "Why am I sitting here listening to this shit?"

"You're like me. You don't want to give her up. You want to figure your way out of this. Like maybe I'm lying or insane or you can buy me off. Or how about this one? Maybe you can get me to say something about her, something so gross that you'll want to get rid of her. That would be freedom for you, right? Because you're not free now, no way, you're enslaved. *En*slaved to the *n*th."

"You have to be nuts," was Harvey's analysis. "First you answer the door, which is not entirely your fault, then you go out for coffee with this man who claims to be Julia's boyfriend. Julia herself tells you it isn't true, yet you're torturing yourself by believing this nutcase over her. What if I tell you I'm putting it to Julia, are you going to believe me too? Look, Martin, this guy is just setting you up. In a day or a week he's going to give you a chance to pay him off. That's what it's all about. Money."

Philip lived "with friends" in a warehouse space just north of the lakeshore. From the south window you could see the lake itself, enclosed on the east by the long finger of the Leslie Street Spit, to the north and west by the islands.

The friends were fashion photographers. Screens, drapes, strobe lights and spots were hung from tracks suspended from the twenty-foot ceiling. One corner was sectioned off as a darkroom: above it was the loft where the photographers slept. Philip showed Martin the sleeping bag that was his bed. Tightly rolled and stuffed into a small nylon sack, it sat waiting for night at the end of the long couch on which Philip sat explaining his philosophy of life as Martin inspected the studio.

"I have a safety deposit box somewhere, I won't tell you in case you get tempted, and every time I make some money I put it away for my retirement. *Radical saving* is what I call my plan: a few high-tech stocks, anything to do with measles vaccine, software companies I've worked for, then your blue chip stuff. Any time you need some advice. Though I don't suppose Julia would be interested in you if you didn't have the financial side covered. Knowing Julia, I mean."

From the darkroom came the bubbling of an espresso machine. Philip went to the door, reappeared a minute later carrying a tray with coffee, cups, small white porcelain bowls of milk and sugar.

"You want to smoke something?" Philip asked. "Now that we're getting to know each other."

After a few weeks Martin moved to a one-room apartment in the east end. He cashed his retirement fund, sold everything but two suitcases of clothes and his passport. His plan was to go to England for the rest of the winter, come back with nothing and start over. But one night in a bar, one of the oyster bars he used to go to, he met an old friend who had become properties manager for a real estate agent. The friend offered Martin a job cleaning the halls and bathrooms of several rooming houses of the type Martin was considering for his next stop on the way to nowhere. Martin cancelled his trip to England. With his first cheque he bought himself an oversize television set. In late March, having had a few beers while watching a crucial hockey game, Martin telephoned Harvey to wish him a happy birthday; Harvey frostily informed him that Julia, after suffering a nervous breakdown through which she managed to hang on to her job, was now rebuilding her life with the help of a sympathetic therapist.

While listening to Harvey, Martin was still keeping an eye on the game, but with the sound muted. After Harvey was finished, Martin opened a new beer and went to the window. The view was grime, street lights and snow. For some reason that comforted him.

It wasn't until he had set his alarm and turned out the lights that Martin began to think about Harvey's final comment: "Some people make something of their lives—others just sink to their own level."

That night Martin dreamed he was in a snowstorm, lost in the centre of the city. The snow was falling to the sound of Beethoven's Sixth and he was searching for Julia. Suddenly Philip appeared, took him by the arm, and explained through the crashing of horns and a rising tide of strings that Julia was waiting for him by the fire. Still in his dream, he woke to find himself in the grey early morning, standing at a downtown corner, his hands out, waiting for passersby. After an hour or two, he looked down at his hands to see how much money he had collected: his gloves were torn and his palms bleeding. He was just beginning to realize he must have been crucified when he awoke again, this time in his sleeping bag on the fold-out couch. His stomach began to churn, the way it did when he used to live with Julia, then the alarm went off and he swung his feet to the floor, stood with the grey-yellow light bathing him in some curious and totally satisfying benediction he knew to be entirely unearned, as unlikely and fleeting as a single perfect note, or the half-remembered touch of Julia's lips against his ribs.

the anatomy
of insects

THE SAME SUMMER William Mills took up dissecting insects, he ordered his eight-year-old son Lawrence to go to his room and change into his bathing suit. Lawrence, believing they were about to go swimming, obeyed. When he returned his father made him stand against the kitchen doorjamb, which had been marked to resemble an oversize ruler. But instead of measuring Lawrence, his father told him to stand still, then took his picture with the Polaroid camera he carried with him when he crawled about the yard or down by the river, photographing insects in "their natural habitat." Lawrence spent the rest of the summer considering two possibilities: first, that his father was trying to tell him that his own "natural habitat" was standing shivering in his bathing suit with his back pressed uncomfortably against a wooden doorjamb; or second, that his father intended to kill him one night in order to dissect him.

Twenty-five years later Amelia would tell Lawrence that his natural home—she didn't use words like habitat—was rented cars. Lawrence assumed Amelia was upset because their last night out had begun with take-out hamburgers followed by a drive-in movie. On the other hand, he was sure Amelia would admit that rented cars had driven them to some wonderful places, fully supplied with scenery and fold-down seats from which they had blasted off to some of their most memorable moments. "I can't buy things like cars and houses," Lawrence tried to explain, "it all has to do with my parents." But even Lawrence understood that Amelia had her own burdens.

At some point in the last few miles the landscape has shifted. A sudden transition Lawrence never expects, never remembers, but it always arrives this way, and once he has come this far, to this place that is home, the loose whirring keys align themselves, lock into position, *thunk*, and suddenly he is whole again, home again, back to the place he is always so eager to escape, so reluctant to return to.

It is November, late afternoon. Lawrence drives the frostbitten blacktop winding through swamp-killed trees until finally the road rises to a grassy ridge spotted with tall pines trembling in the grey light. He is back in his own country, known rhythms of wind. In this cold, his bare fingers wrapped around the steering wheel look naked and vulnerable. The pines fall away and the road goes down again, this time into a long stretch of white-tipped marsh grass already crippled by November nights. Just looking out is enough to let him feel the hard welcome of frozen ground banging into the workboots he once wore, hear the sharp rustling of grassy stalks against his legs as he strides into the woods, smell the sweet fallen leaves and bark and north winds getting ready to tie you down for winter, whip you with snow, send you into a deep freeze where no one can hear you calling out for mouth-to-mouth inspiration.

Mouth-to-mouth inspiration. Sometimes Lawrence wishes he had an editor resident in his brain, an optimistic gnom-ette to keep him on the straight and narrow. Or maybe it should be the other way around: he could be the gnome, let the brain belong to someone else. This thought pleases Lawrence because, in fact, it has a certain truth. He *is* the gnome, the self-appointed sceptical, sarcastic, censorious and sometimes senseless voice speaking into the centre of the nation's collective brain. Or at least that was the idea.

On the seat beside him is a tape recorder with a long thin wire leading to the microphone Lawrence now holds in his hand, bringing it close to his mouth as though he is a rock singer about to exhale a hormone hurricane.

As the millennium approached, it became increasingly clear that humanity was gripped by a mass psychosis. Computer games, tele-vision shows and movies, even comic books offered endless variations on the theme of doom-obsessed nuts inflicting horrifying damage on themselves and everyone around them. Articles began to spring up in financial pages about the amounts of money to be made in such movies and games. A couple of business school students even started a mutual fund, "Apocalypse Futures" that specialized in a combination of horror entertainment investments and pharmaceu-tical companies that manufactured chemical warfare nightmares.

Lawrence switched off his tape recorder. *Chemical warfare nightmares.* Who was going to believe that? Those who manufactured or invested in closely engineered devices designed to dissolve you from the inside out, or turn your brain into a mall parking lot after a flash flood, were probably not among the apparently ever-sparser group who listened to *The Lawrence Mills News Digest*, as his show was called. At one time he had taken that show on the road every year, hopping from campus to campus across the country, broadcasting for a week from each of two dozen student cafeterias and auditoriums where he'd be surrounded by the curious, the converts, the earnest young journalism students and campus politicos.

But over the last ten years the vicious circle of budget chops leading to travel cuts, reduced format, deteriorations in production staff and time slot had flushed him into a shrinking universe that would eventually spit him out into the black hole of silence.

Even now he was a curiosity. *Lawrence Mills? You used to be Lawrence Mills? I listened to you every Thursday night for years...* As though he was now someone else entirely, a seedy impostor who had stolen the name of a favourite old song. *You used to be Lawrence Mills?* And then he would speak. He still had the voice. The pipes. In his heyday he had cared for them like a violinist nursing his grandfather's Stradivarius: eight hours' sleep a night, no hard liquor except on weekends, no smoke other than water-cooled plus a single weekly cigar while he made the final cut.

A pair of headlights appeared behind him from nowhere. His sudden rush of fear popped as the lights swerved out to pass. The car was a sleek limousine-style Cadillac, the driver a man his own age wearing a leather jacket, an open-necked sports shirt. His dark hair was brushed back in silver-tipped wings that made his aquiline nose look too big for his face. He grinned at Lawrence, as though he knew Lawrence was staring at him jealously, then accelerated so Lawrence was first left with the red vertical tail lights, then nothing at all as the Cadillac sped around a curve and out of sight.

Lawrence flicked on the tape recorder. *Mass psychosis was the easy explanation. What no one suspected was that the entire human unconscious was being shaped not by common fears about the future, but by an entirely different agency, a force entirely beyond human control that had—possibly from the very birth of mankind—been playing humanity's collective soul with virtuoso ease, I am talking here about the obvious, the malignant alien evil force that . . .*

The fact was, Lawrence realized, the fact was, the fact. The Fact. There was no fact. Fact, what a word. Fact if I know, Lawrence said to himself, that's a good one. In fact I'm not even old, only pitiful. *Stop whining.* Now the cars were coming towards him in a steady stream. Night was, as were they, falling.

In this week's personal essay, I would like to reflect on the Nation's Capital. As the visitor approaches it from the outside, possibly in a rented car, he sees a long line of vehicles departing what was once the heart of our country. Let us say it is nightfall. Falling like the curtain at the end of a play we have all enjoyed but now know has come to its conclusion. Goodbye, Canada, the actors call out softly. By now, unfortunately, most of the audience is in the lobby searching for their coats, ready to grab a taxi for some more entertaining place. The few believers who remain clap as loudly as they can, but in the almost empty theatre they can't raise enough of an ovation to get an encore. The fact is, if there are any facts in this strange case of a country that disappeared, fact if I know, the few hangers-on might as well go around the back and meet the players for a drink. Time to forget about encores, time to drown the bitterness of a last performance given to an empty hall . . .

Lawrence rewound his tape and began to listen. Suddenly his car lit up like the brain of some victim who had swallowed a ten-billion-watt anti-personnel oblivion pill.

The high beams of a transport were bathing him in a piss-yellow light filled with the loud blare of its horn. Meanwhile cars were coming towards him in an unbroken line. Now that night had fallen, as they say, *bam!*, there was nothing but the headlights in his eyes, the high beams from behind, the approaching halogen oasis of a mini-plaza. Lawrence looked at his dashboard. While talking to his tape recorder he had slowed to forty kilometres an hour. He stamped the accelerator to the floor. His rented car hesitated briefly while the automatic transmission drowned itself, then began to speed up. He had just put a tolerable space between himself and the transport headlights when from under the hood he heard a definitive *pop!* as though a large piece of popcorn had just flowered: at the same time there emerged from his hood a glowing red piece of metal "about the size of a cheerleader's baton" he would later say, which took off at a leftward angle and disappeared from sight. The engine began to make terrible clacking, grinding, and metallic self-chewing sounds while the car bucked and swerved irregularly as he struggled to get it off the road.

"Good of you to come." His father answered the door in his wheelchair, then spun away with unexpected dexterity as Lawrence stepped into the map room. *The map room.* On various occasions Lawrence had tried to explain the map room to would-be gnomettes, though they didn't always know the details of the job they didn't know they were being interviewed for. As might be expected, the map room contained the whole world, but in no particular order.

At this moment Lawrence isn't looking, he's smelling. A thick cheesy odour cut with hamburger and tomato sauce.

"Smells great," Lawrence says. "Sorry I'm late. My car exploded."

He is speaking to the back of his father's head, a wide strangely horizontal oval with ears that cling to its sides and a cover of sparse sandy hair. The unsettling sideways look of the head is emphasized by the narrow neck beneath, which itself seems insecurely attached to the bony shoulders. For the occasion his father is wearing a clean shirt and the cardigan Lawrence's mother gave him decades ago.

"I've made your favourite, meat loaf with cheese," William Mills says, turning towards Lawrence again. His face, like the back of his head, spreads out from top to bottom. His wide jaws, Lawrence now notices, are clean-shaven, and as he speaks and smiles his mouth stretches and brackets itself with the dimples everyone always notices in the photographs.

Lawrence's father is a special case. A voice virtuoso in his own right, William Mills sealed his fate with a single anonymous phone call after Lawrence left home to go to university. Until then his family had appeared ideally normal. The kind of family you might see on television, his father used to say. Though Lawrence wondered if television family fathers kept a set of razor-sharp scalpels stored in a plastic lunchbox on top of the medicine chest of the basement bathroom. In their television family, Lawrence was the self-conscious bespectacled high-school student who tried to build his confidence and meet girls by joining the radio club. William, the comically over-serious father, was a government bureaucrat who lost harmlessly insignificant amounts of money speculating on gold mines, and indulged a strange liking for cold cuts generously slathered with curried mustard. Lawrence's mother, Laura, was the reluctantly modern woman who worked as assistant manager of a mall bake shop. At that time there were no wheelchairs in the family. Shortly after Lawrence left home, Laura Mills began wearing grey suits with white shirts. Sometimes she had to go to seminars. A year later she was promoted to an administrative office in Montreal.

It took Lawrence a long time to figure out that by moving from Ottawa to Montreal, his mother had left his father. William was faster off the mark. A few months after his wife moved he drove down to Montreal and let himself into his wife's apartment with the key he'd secretly copied during a weekend visit. The apartment was empty of people but littered with "evidence," as he later told the judge: male underwear, razor and shaving cream, a half-finished bottle of rum—which he knew Laura detested—along with a half-eaten pizza in the refrigerator.

The fateful phone call: disguising his voice William called his wife and announced he was in her apartment doing various disgusting things and was hoping she would return to share even more adventurous pleasures, which he referred to in some detail. Pleased with himself, he hung up. As William later explained in court, it never occurred to him that instead of ignoring the call, or perhaps even realizing it was him and going home to "face the music," she would telephone the police. In fact, if facts exist, what he did after the phone call was to take a shower because it was a hot summer day and the two-hour drive from Ottawa had left him sour and sweaty. It was only while returning to Ottawa, after the humiliating and perhaps terrifying experience of having the police pull back the plastic gull-imprinted shower curtain while he was scrubbing his wife's—or perhaps her lover's—shampoo into his hair, that he had the accident which led to the wheelchair.

After dinner, Lawrence did the dishes while William worked on his latest needlepoint, an exact copy of *Northern Pines* by Tom Thomson. *Dutiful son obsessively cleans family crockery*, Lawrence imagined himself intoning. Watching the frantic movements of his hand trying to scrub smooth the bottom of the lasagna pan, he thought of his mother, now out of the food business and working as a dispatcher for a Montreal taxi company. Competent, immersed, a master weaver and navigator of social webs, his mother had left them both, he finally realized, because she'd stopped being able to believe in these strange isolated men entirely caught up in maintaining their cocoons.

He slept on the living room pull-out couch, as he always did when he visited his father. Going to bed he anticipated a long restless night—usually on these visits he ended up awake and dressed by six—but instead awoke to a bright blue morning. His father had wheeled to his bedside, and was drinking coffee and looking down at him as if it were the old days again and he was getting ready to dissect.

Lawrence closed his eyes. For some reason he found it easy to believe his father was balancing a scalpel in his palm, and that smoothed onto his lap was a map of the human thorax with arrows pointing directions to the heart. *Questioned by police, William Mills explained that he was merely trying to discover his son's true feelings.* The way he had explained to police, that time in Montreal, that he was in the shower because he always liked to cleanse himself before a ritual killing. "Just joking," he later told the judge, "I thought they were French and wouldn't understand me."

"I thought we'd go out to the cemetery this morning," William announced while Lawrence struggled out from under the covers.

"What cemetery?"

"I'm buying a plot. I thought you should look at the possible options since you're the only one who's ever going to visit me."

"Millennial paranoia," Lawrence said, walking towards the bathroom. He could hear the squeak of the wheelchair turning to follow, the smooth hum of its tires on the hardwood floor. He peed with his back to the door, where his father still waited, then began preparing to shave. "Millennial paranoia, it's my next program. My theory is that because of the millennium, everyone feels free to indulge their secret belief that the world is about to end. Your more narcissistic types, the ones who believe they *are* the whole world, become convinced they're about to die. They buy insurance and cemetery plots..."

Now Lawrence turned from the mirror and saw that his father did indeed have a map on his lap. Not of his chest or an insect thorax, but of something called Allpine Memorial Grounds. It looked, in fact, if facts there were, like a gated subdivision, complete with straight streets, curved crescents, areas stamped FULL or UNDER DEVELOPMENT.

"Maybe you'd rather have me cremated," his father said. "I hear a lot of children like to keep the ashes now, as souvenirs. Or you could scatter me somewhere, if that would make you feel better."

Amelia: she was, Lawrence could never decide which, either the rainbow after the storm or the sliver under the fingernail.

"All right," she said, when Lawrence phoned to announce that his father was dead. "I suppose you had no one else to tell."

In her voice Lawrence could hear two distinct elements: cold indifference and genuine sympathy. He could have told her so but similar intuitions had never been popular. In fact, if fact there was, they hadn't spoken for six months, and so during the silence following her reaction Lawrence wondered if cold indifference might not be all that was left of their relationship, while the genuine sympathy was directed towards his father, who in addition to dying had been saddled with having Lawrence Mills as his only surviving heir.

"I told my mother," Lawrence said.

"How was that?"

"Not so good."

"I wish he'd killed himself in the car," his mother had said. "Don't expect me at the funeral."

"I don't," Lawrence replied. There wasn't going to be a funeral. His plan was a cremation ceremony, after which he had hoped his mother would take away the ashes.

"Any plans to come and visit?" his mother then asked. "Or don't you visit your mother any more?"

"She's a strange one, your mother," Amelia said.

Now the genuine sympathy outweighed the cold indifference. Hearing these warm tones in Amelia's voice made Lawrence's eyes hurt, as though they wanted to cry.

Later that night, Amelia pulled his head down so it was cradled between her breasts. They had her duvet pulled over them, into the tent under which Amelia liked to make love, and Lawrence again felt his eyes filling, straining to release. He was on the edge of dissolving into tears, he was imagining himself dissolving into tears, he was thinking how wonderful it would be if he could just cross the invisible line and actually weep, he was thinking how typical it was of him to be unable to make the step into real emotion and finally he was thinking that at least he had brought himself to the brink when Amelia accidentally brought her unshaven November shin up between his legs and the sweet dissolve he had planned turned into a sharp cry of pain followed by a gush of tears during which he thought of his father trapped in his car, his legs already paralyzed, realizing, as he'd related to Lawrence, "that this accident could be my big chance to get off the karma wheel."

"You cried," Amelia said. She was cradling his pain in her hands and Lawrence wished he had a diamond ring or some other guarantee. Then the pain drained away and he was just a body, lying under the benevolent duvet tent of his sometimes girlfriend.

A year later, Lawrence was again driving towards Ottawa. Another November, another rented car. Snow was falling, a dry gritty snow that collected along his wipers and the edges of his windshield. When he reached the spot where the pines fell away and the highway dipped into a stretch of frozen marsh grass, this year half buried in snow, he stopped the car. In the back seat was a large ceramic vase stoppered by a sturdy cork sealed with a thin layer of red wax. Before picking it up, Lawrence switched on the tape recorder.

On the anniversary of the first of my programs about universal evil, the alien agency that has twisted and darkened . . .

Lawrence paused. Since the *Lawrence Mills News Digest* had begun to carry his bi-weekly essays on alien evil, his show had developed a new and growing group of listeners.

He now spent hours every week tending to his Web site, and the syndicate had added eighteen new stations. Letters poured in, including invitations to science fiction conferences, revivalist gatherings, associations dedicated to the paranormal. The digest now had an Internet address, a busy Web page complete with several linked shrines. His rented car had progressed from Rent-A-Wreck to a leased semi-luxury Japanese four-wheel drive with air conditioning, heated driver's seat, and a specially installed eight-speaker sound system that sounded like Carnegie Hall on drugs.

Lawrence took the stoppered vase and got out of the car. From the back he withdrew the plastic shovel he had bought to use in the unlikely event his amazing all-terrain vehicle actually got stuck. A few minutes later he had crossed the frozen marsh and was following a narrow winding creek through a stretch of scrubby brush. When he reached an opening he stood for a moment, short of breath, the cold air catching at his lungs. He cradled the vase in his arms, holding it against his chest as though it were a baby he was trying to keep warm. The snow had stopped. The western rim of the sky was tinged with yellow and red. Above, the clouds had broken up, and patches of weak grey-blue held the last of the light.

"This is it," Lawrence said. He walked until he was facing a large granite outcropping. The massive slab of rock stared at him implacably. Or expectantly. "I suppose this is the kind of occasion that requires a few words," Lawrence admitted. "No problem, I am a professional, after all."

He was reminded that, on the *Lawrence Mills News Digest*, no mention had yet been made of his father's passing. "Friends, Romans, countrymen," Lawrence addressed the rock. "In the twenty years of my broadcasts to you, I have made it a policy to exclude details of my personal life. In fact, if facts there are, *fact if I know*, my own life is quite boring. Perhaps because I have given it over to serving you, whoever you are, a few discerning members of the public to be found in better stores everywhere, or perhaps because the fact is that I am a total asshole, utterly boring, and though unable to change my own deeply flawed inner self have at least refrained from inflicting it on others. With a few exceptions. You know who you are.

"Today, I stand before you, exceptionally, to announce that one of those exceptions—at times, I'll admit it, I thought he was the most important exception of all—is no longer with us. Gone. He wanted to be gone. He stuffed himself with poison and died in a disgusting pool of his own vomit and blood. But I come not to praise Caesar. Nor to bury him. He would have liked to be buried but, to tell the truth, if truth there is, I didn't want to bury him. I didn't want to think about his body—a body he arranged I would be the one to discover—rotting away in its coffin. Or even being preserved in his coffin. Oh yes, the flesh men have is oft interred with their bones—*but not this time*. Now, all that remains, all *the* remains, are in this vase. Bones, ashes, a bit of burn-off gas."

Having started, Lawrence realized he had a lot to say. His eyes had that familiar over-full stinging sensation, but Amelia's breasts were not available to console him.

"Now that he's dead, I'm going it alone," Lawrence announced. There were marks on the granite that could be construed as faces. "If I wanted to," Lawrence said, "I could decide you were faces."

He contemplated this possibility. "In the end," Lawrence said, "you make a terrible audience but a perfect wall. The proverbial wall." Lawrence was inspecting this wall when suddenly something of enormous significance came into his mind. "The secret of the evil empire is time," Lawrence said aloud. He gave a nervous laugh but it sounded foolish in the cold. "The secret of the evil empire is time," he said again and remembered the early days of the *Lawrence Mills News Digest* when everything he said was so *true* that he expected to be struck down as he spoke. Then the wind swirled and he felt as though he were in a roofless elevator accelerating towards the lead ceiling that used to be the future.

He was holding his father's remains and he was shivering. His intention had been to uncork the vase and spread the ashes on the snow. "This is the viewing of the corpse," he had been going to announce. After that he had imagined himself pouring out the ashes in the shape of a stick figure. "Goodbye," he might have said, then covered the ashes with snow: the burial his father had refused.

But now the cork wouldn't come out. It was frozen or stuck or reluctant for other obvious reasons. Suddenly Lawrence remembered the Polaroid photograph his father had taken of him when he was eight years old, standing skinny and frightened against the kitchen doorjamb. A surge of anger swept through him—it made a noise like hard flint shooting sparks.

Lawrence took a few steps back from the wall. Then he hurled the vase into the rock. It shattered with a loud unexpected crack, as though it had exploded. A piece of the pottery—or, he later thought, perhaps a jagged edge of bone—caught him on the left cheek, opening a painful gash. He pressed some snow to his cheek, then took it away to inspect. His blood had made a long dark oblong in the snow. He held it close to his mouth, as though it were a microphone. *Father, this is Lawrence Mills. I'm using my blood to connect us up, the way we always were. I know you're moving on to your next incarnation now. But just before we lose touch altogether, I just want to say that I paid a lot more attention to you than you did to me. Think about it.*

He bled the whole way back to the car. He knew he would stop at the first telephone and call Amelia, to ask her to marry him. But he couldn't have forecast the feeling it gave him when she agreed, the way it grew from one of completeness to wild exuberance as he drove towards her singing songs he forgot as quickly as he made them up, tapping his foot on the accelerator and hugging the steering wheel, so that his car danced with him through the night.

literary

synapses

IBECAME PRIVATE SECRETARY to Stephen Leacock, the famed Canadian humorist, purely by chance. He was sitting at his usual table at the bar of the Ritz, a quick cab ride away from McGill University where he was employed and I was not. The bar was in semi-darkness. Feeling the muse upon him, Professor Leacock had surrounded his table with banana peels to ensure his privacy while he composed a lecture entitled, as I will never forget, "The Comedy of Thomas Hobbes."

In those years Stephen Leacock's picture was often in the newspaper: I recognized him at once. The bushy hair, the generous moustache, the red drinker's cheeks and the jolly sparkle in his eyes as he watched me approach. In fact I did not mean to be approaching him directly, it was just that his table happened to be next to the gentlemen's washroom.

"My mother's a great admirer of yours," I was about to say. Then my right foot hit the outer ring of banana peels and I flipped into the air.

When Leacock had finished wiping the tears of laughter from his eyes he apologized profusely, and insisted on buying me a drink.

"Hobbes himself was a great prankster," Leacock explained to me, once I'd settled in and he'd gotten his famous meerschaum going with great puffing towards the ceiling. "He was notorious for inviting his friends to his club, Hobbes was a great club-goer you know, and then having the kitchen serve them sausages spiked with powerful emetics."

As I tried to contain my gusts of hilarity, Leacock patted my shoulder concernedly. "You have heard of Thomas Hobbes, haven't you?"

By coincidence I had just completed a forty-page essay on the Oedipal subtext of Hobbes' subservience to liberal economic theory. Still shaking with laughter, I was unable to manage such a mouthful, and contented myself with gasping out, "Hobbes, yes, life . . . nasty . . . brutish . . . short."

At this Leacock fairly exploded. Strange though it may seem, this joke I made so early in our acquaintance was the only time I managed to come up with a statement sufficiently witty to cause Professor Leacock to fall off his chair and lose his breath to the extent that an ambulance was required.

While sitting by his hospital bed I helped him compose the Hobbes lecture—surely the least I could do under the circumstances—and as a result he offered me part-time work as his assistant, a job that became, for a certain period, my entire life.

Of course people will be curious to know what it was like to work with the great man. I had thought, given our first meeting, that my employment would consist mainly of going to the Ritz and other such places with the professor where we would try to injure each other with jokes. Perhaps there would also be a certain amount of research to aid him with his academic endeavours. I was wrong. Professor Leacock had hired me for one and only one reason: to witness, record and help him conduct the numerous love affairs in which he was secretly engaged.

No one could have been more eager for this task: I had no such distractions of my own but was fervently hoping to learn the necessary lessons from the professor. Eventually—although this story properly belongs elsewhere and I mention it here only to give credit where it is due—I assimilated enough of Professor Leacock's techniques that, to give just one example of my later effect on the so-called fair sex, when I stood up to lecture in his place on the political economy of bandages to a class of nurses, my very appearance was greeted with spontaneous laughter.

Stephen Leacock, being the man he was, had interests much wider than humoristic stories and political science. When he greeted me one day with the question: "What is the best opening line in all of literature?" I knew something on the order of "It was a dark and stormy night..." or "Many people have boasted about their dogs but I think I may safely say..." would not suffice.

With Professor Leacock being the genius he was, there was no point in trying to out-reason him. I therefore let instinct be my guide and replied, "She got in and put her suitcase on the rack, and the brace of pheasants on top of it."

Leacock turned pale. "How did you know?"

I grasped his hand and stared at it. "I read it in your palm," I said. Although that wasn't the answer. How *had* I known? It was just a lucky guess.

Leacock tore his hand away in disgust. "And what's the last line of that story?"

"Just a moment," I said. "You have to admit, Professor

Leacock, that answering your initial question was no small feat."

"Yes, yes," he grumbled. "*No small feat*, as you say." He began to embroider. "'Asked a difficult question upon arriving at his employer's door, the secretary, a man of *no small feat*, was able to reply—' How's that?"

"Excellent, sir."

"And how would you continue?"

"I have no idea. Sir."

"Try."

"But Professor Leacock, for me to continue what you have begun . . . talk about pinning the tale on the donkey."

As the umbrella stand came crashing down on my skull I realized that the professor had heard "tail" rather than "tale" thus inferring I had called him, rather than myself, a donkey. That, of course, is the problem with humorists: they are tremendously literal-minded, as well as being, of course, only interested in their own jokes.

As soon as I was bandaged up, Leacock returned to his first line of attack.

"Prove to me it wasn't a lucky guess. Tell me the last line."

"Very well, Professor." We were seated in his library— Leacock in his famous Stephen Leacock Chair of Political Economy, I on a perfectly comfortable wooden stool at the small desk he'd had installed so I could record his off-the-cuff witticisms. "But did she, all the same, as she opened the carriage door and stepped out, murmur 'Chk. Chk,' as she passed?"

"Would you mind repeating that?"

"But did she, all the same, as she opened the carriage door and stepped out, murmur 'Chk. Chk,' as she passed," I repeated.

Leacock leaned back, a contented smile playing across his features.

"She has, you must admit, a sublime way with words."

He was speaking of Virginia Woolf, from whose story "The Shooting Party" the quotations are drawn. For a moment we sat in silence, sipping at our drinks.

"I would never have married Virginia Woolf," Stephen Leacock said.

"I know what you mean." And I said that, not simply to encourage him in his conversation, but because I did sincerely find it difficult to imagine the two of them together. Now I see my blindness as a kind of literary snobbery that I hope my life experience has helped me overcome. In any case, Professor Leacock took offence.

"So you think she's too good for me!" he said softly. There was hurt in his tone, anger too. I shouldn't have been surprised, at that moment, had he drawn a sword from his umbrella and challenged me to a duel. Instead he gulped down his drink and poured himself another. "Do you mind if I speak French?"

"Of course not," I said.

He began to speak quickly in French. My job included recording even our most casual conversations—"You have to save the good bits," he had admonished me early on, "otherwise you can't make the stew"—but my notes for that moment show only an illegible scrawl.

"Do you understand French?" he asked.

"A little," I said. I was a newcomer to Montreal, but had picked up a smattering of the language after the war, when we lived next door to a family of French refugees from Lyon. The little neighbour girl and I would sometimes go into the garage, take off our clothes and flip a coin to see who was going to be the occupying army. Professor Leacock's French, naturally, bore no resemblance to the kinds of noises we used to make.

"There was a certain thing I wished to say to M. Flaubert," was one of the sentences I managed to get down. Another: "Charles mistook the back of the limousine for the little corner." Only recently did I come to understand the significance of this. Unfortunately all that followed and preceded it has been lost.

The first year I worked for him, Stephen Leacock's principal extramarital liaison was with Harriet Taylor—the famous early feminist writer who eventually married John Stuart Mill, Hobbes's heir and Stephen Leacock's predecessor.

John Stuart Mill's grave is to be found in a cemetery outside Avignon, the French city renowned for its bridge and its popes. During a certain period, a well-known local entomologist called Jean-Henri Fabre, a great admirer of Mill, used to visit that grave and speculate on the exact details of the relationship between the former Mrs. Taylor, whose first husband was a kindly but uncultivated gentleman, and the eminent political theorist. It was after Mr. Taylor's death that Mrs. Taylor became Mrs. Mill, and after Mr. Leacock's death that I happened across a photograph of J.-H. Fabre gazing contemplatively, a bouquet of mimosas in his hand, at John Stuart Mill's final resting place.

Where Harriet Taylor was buried, I do not know. But she was safely ensconced before Stephen Leacock became involved with her. The affair required, therefore, a third party: Mrs. Emily Fairbanks, who in addition to being the sister of the swashbuckling actor, claimed to be the clairvoyant who advised Mackenzie King's psychic and who in fact had done the hard spadework of actually digging up his mother.

Mrs. Fairbanks did not shrink from her role. She would arrive at Professor Leacock's door on the stroke of midnight, her heavily lipsticked lips invariably parted in a broad grin, as though to say, "We all know this is a farce, but let's be good sports and play our parts to the hilt. Someone might be watching."

Just inside the professor's door had been installed, as in many such houses, a powder room for the comfort of the guests. Having given me her ample but ratty fur, Mrs. Fairbanks would retire for a full fifteen minutes. When she emerged she would be wearing a dark star-spotted turban, a red wraparound dress, heavy gold jewellery of the type that might have been given to her by an infatuated pirate who had robbed Consumers' Distributing. Her elaborate red lips, her scimitar nose, her black eyebrows that looked to be coated with shoe polish, her large white teeth that protruded slightly as she greeted the professor and extended one be-ringed hand for his lips while in the other she held the as-she-called-it heavenly sphere itself.

The ritual then demanded that we pass into the dining room. While Mrs. Fairbanks took her place at the head of the table and busied herself with arranging the candles, etc., my job was to prepare tea in the kitchen. A platter would have been readied before my arrival—all I had to do was boil the water and add it to the teaball already waiting in the pot.

There was a problem about holding hands at the table. I needed my hands for taking notes. It was decided that in this emergency situation, feet could substitute. And so we all took off our shoes and went foot-to-foot-to-foot.

Mrs. Fairbanks, her broad handsome face wavering in the candlelight, would then emit a few suitably introductory words. "Once again this evening will we be making our way down the astral highways . . ." or "In our voyage across the cosmic seas of life and time this evening . . ." Meanwhile Professor Leacock, normally so serene and poised, would start to fidget.

Gradually the sphere, upon which the candlelight played, would begin to glow from within. We would lean forward eagerly, trying to see in its depths the initial outlines of some face or silhouette. During this period Mrs. Fairbanks' eyes would be tightly closed. "I hear a voice," she would say, or, "There's whispering, but I don't understand the language," or, "I believe this one's speaking French," or, finally, "Now I'm getting her." Mrs. Fairbanks' face would gradually go blank before beginning to take on the features of the communicating spirit, until her own physiognomy was virtually identical to the one we saw within the ball. Her voice had the same tendency, so that when, for example, Virginia Woolf herself appeared, she spoke in the delightful high-pitched tinkle of the British upper classes.

"Why, Stephen! How delightful! And you're looking so well!"

From what I'd read of her books along with the one-page biographies on their backs, I would have expected Virginia Woolf to be a very sad woman, bulked up with lumpy sweaters, her suicide, her affair with Vita Sackville-West and, above all, the chains of her famous melancholy. Like most men, I suppose—of course to this stereotype as most others Professor Leacock was an exception—I admired the felicity of her prose but my admiration was fully matched by the pity I felt for poor Leonard about whom the cover copy always said "in 1912 she consented to marry Leonard Woolf." What was that supposed to mean? Why couldn't she have just "married Leonard Woolf" like anyone else? But of course she couldn't, could she, do things like anyone else. *She* was Virginia Woolf. It was like being the Queen, but you didn't get an income and your tea service was cracked. As can be seen this line about having "consented to marry" had set me entirely against her.

So what a surprise she was!

While Mrs. Fairbanks, eyes tightly closed, became round and jolly of feature, Professor Leacock, his own eyes closed, trembled with the effort of speaking in tones he must have felt suitably refined for dialogue with Mrs. Woolf. I would be taking notes—eyes open of course—and therefore could look at Virginia Woolf herself, as she sat quite convincingly materialized two chairs down from me at the dining-room table.

Slender, neatly dressed in a dark red tailored suit with a shawl around her shoulders, about forty years old with excellent though slightly mannish features, luminous—at least in the candlelight—and endowed with an extraordinarily attractive and intelligent mouth, Virginia Woolf made a most impressive apparition. One conversation, for which I still have the notes lest anyone doubt its authenticity, proceeded thusly:

MRS. FAIRBANKS: Virginia. Yes. I feel you are with us, Virginia.

VIRGINIA WOOLF (who was on this occasion wearing her suit as always, but instead of a shawl a long purple-and-gold scarf that she kept winding nervously about her fingers, perhaps puzzled that Mrs. Fairbanks, after all the trouble she'd gone to to fetch her, refused to open her eyes to the obvious): Yes, I am here, Mrs. Fairbanks. How are you this evening?

MRS. FAIRBANKS: I am very well, Virginia. What messages do you have for us from the great universal spheres, the deep unutterable cosmos?

VIRGINIA WOOLF (winking at me and cupping her hands around her mouth): Oooooooooaaaooooooh, Ooooooo-aaaaooooooh, Oooooaahhh, Wawawawawawawawaaaaaaaah yehhhhhhhs Misssusss Fehrbaaaaanks, I seee, yessss, I seeee your great-great-Uncle Thomas. . . .

MRS. FAIRBANKS (her closed eyes beginning to brim with tears): Yes, Virginia, tell me, please, is it ver-ry hor-rible?

VIRGINIA WOOLF (looking at me and rolling her eyes as only she could): Still tied to the stake, Mrs. Fairbanks. I'm so terribly sorry. The fire is burning, there are dozens of little red devils dancing around him, poking him with pitchforks, it's horrid, Mrs. Fairbanks . . .

MRS. FAIRBANKS (on the verge of fainting): Is he in pain?

VIRGINIA WOOLF: Terrible pain. And yet he is ever so brave, yes, he's trying to protect, yes, I see it, a little address book he has in his frock . . .

MRS. FAIRBANKS: He was a priest, you know, until—

VIRGINIA WOOLF: No, it's poetry. Now he's beginning to read . . . I can hear him, yes, listen, Mrs. Fairbanks, listen, can you hear him?

MRS. FAIRBANKS: Yes, but I can't quite make out the words . . .

Eventually, of course, the exchanges would take place between Virginia Woolf and Stephen Leacock. Despite my initial snap judgment, I quickly came to realize my error: these two were ideally suited to each other and it was, in at least my view, one of the great tragedies of both British and Canadian letters that time and geography prevented this "marriage of true minds." Imagine how much better off Virginia Woolf would have been if, instead of having "consented to marry" the in-all-ways worthy and brilliant but also dour and all-too-serious Leonard Woolf, she'd been with Stephen Leacock. Every time she stepped out to drown herself—and it should be added that Montreal provides only a very short season for such unhappy possibilities— she would have been distracted by having to watch out for the banana peels Leacock liked to scatter about with the prodigal genius with which, to make a poor comparison, French dogs leave their mark on the streets of Paris. But then, why would she have done such a thing? Life with Stephen Leacock would have been studded with cruises on the *Mariposa Belle*, disastrous attempts to go to the bank, etc. As Professor Leacock recounted these adventures to her, his heel all the time grinding into the arch of my foot, Virginia Woolf would be teary with laughter. I remember one night in particular, I myself so carried away with the hilarity that my notes were skimpier than they should have been, when Leacock told the famous story about how he mistakenly buried his father alive in cement when he only meant to be playing a practical joke on the paper boy. Mrs. Fairbanks, shrieking with laughter, kept crying out "Oh, I'm pressing my knees together! I'm pressing my knees together!" which, added to the comedy of Leacock describing the look of horror on his mother's face as she realized what had happened to Dad, had Virginia Woolf pounding my shoulder with glee—two days later I was covered in giant violet bruises. I myself got the hiccups so badly I had to drink rye backwards out of my glass. Even Leacock himself, rightly renowned for being able to keep a straight face while those about him dissolved in the comedy of it all, couldn't help cracking a smile when he described how he'd broken all of his father's bones sledgehammering him free from his concrete costume.

Of course the humour lay not in the circumstance, as can be seen from my disappointing relation of it, but in the telling. That was one of the many facets of Professor Leacock's great genius. But with Virginia Woolf at his side, in this ideal but impossible marriage of which I was speaking, Leacock's vision could have broadened, deepened, even lengthened. His subject matter might have become, in the sympathetic glow of her presence, not merely the vicissitudes of everyday life, but the rise and fall of empires, the tragedies and comedies of the great, the universal mythology of mankind—in brief, why has Stephen Leacock not become a contemporary Shakespeare? Why is the whole world quoting a long-dead Englishman who lived in the insignificant town of Stratford-on-Avon when the innate and intensely human comedy of Leacock's Orillia-on-Lake-Simcoe could be the lens through which life on this planet is seen? Why has Stephen Leacock not provided, just to give an example, the tone and language for the next translation of the Bible? With Virginia Woolf at his side, such ambitions would have been, I am now convinced, easily fulfilled.

One afternoon we were on the train, Stephen Leacock and I, travelling from Montreal to Toronto for an address he was to give to the Empire Club. As we sat in the first-class coach, watching our country whizz by and sipping from the endless supply of drinks that white-coated porters brought us in both official languages, Leacock had a sudden urge to smoke cigarettes rather than his usual pipe.

Although these were usually sold in our own service, the supply of Leacock's brand had been used up. I began walking through the train to the bar car to see if they could do better.

I hadn't realized how cramped my legs were. It felt good to stretch them, to be moving alone though the swaying train, to stand at the counter of the second class bar surrounded by smoke and silence.

"You going far?" a man asked me. This was in the days when most trains heading west from Montreal continued on to Vancouver.

"Just Toronto," I said.

He nodded. He was wearing one of those orange mustard suits favoured by commercial travellers of the period. His hands were on the bar, large plain hands that looked to have spent a lot of time outdoors.

"Working?"

"Yes," I said.

His face, like his hands, was large and unpretentious. He took out a pack of cigarettes, expertly pushed it open, offered me one although I was already smoking. As he lit up and began to squint against the smoke his expression changed. His eyes narrowed with cunning, as though he was considering some wild proposition. I could imagine him in a Stephen Leacock story. He would be the laughable dupe, the character who thought himself a fox, but was so naive and honest that in the end he was cheated out of what little he had.

"You?" I asked.

He gave me a wide grin. "Got a horse farm in Alberta. Two hundred and fourteen wild mustangs." I tried to imagine this man in his mustard plaids, riding wild mustangs.

Meanwhile he had stepped back and was appraising me. "You look like a bit of a rider. Ever think of giving it all up and coming out west to break horses?" He rubbed his big hands together, then bounced his fist off the bar to request another drink. With a practised swipe he reached up to his neck, loosened his tie and undid the top button of his shirt. "Yup. You'd be great. Probably break a few bones the first day but after that you'd be fine. What did you say you do?"

"I'm a private secretary."

This stopped him. He leaned forward, considered me gravely.

"Well," he finally said, "I'm not going to ask you 'where's your skirt?' because I guess you've heard that one before."

At that point I might have mentioned that in fact I was secretary to the world-famous Canadian humorist, the one who wrote the one about the bank. Or if he'd "heard that one before" there was the one about the banana peels. I might even have asked him if he'd ever heard of, or for that matter gotten married to, the famous prairie poetess, Sarah Binks. But I didn't. Instead I offered my hand for the mustang cowboy to crush, then—my unfinished beer in one hand, a pack of cigarettes in the other—I started back towards the club car. After a couple of minutes the train slowed for its Kingston stop. I got out on the platform for a little fresh air. I was still standing there, drinking my beer and smoking a cigarette, when the train began to pull out of the station. My father had come to his unfortunate end leaping onto a moving train just outside of Leningrad, and I was unwilling to meet the same fate. A few seconds later the club car arrived. Professor Leacock was looking out the window. In one hand was a drink, with the other he was idly twirling the tip of his famous moustache. I cannot say what was in his mind. Perhaps he was ruminating on our last session with Mrs. Fairbanks: at the end of this evening, our toes literally soaked after clutching throughout a particularly exciting encounter with Virginia Woolf during which we had gone tobogganing, Mrs. Fairbanks had turned to Professor Leacock and said, "Sir, you are quite the *most* magnetic man I have ever encountered." After we had seen her out the door Leacock detained me and asked my interpretation of her statement.

"I suppose sir, she might mean, that in the matter of these unusual evenings, you are 'magnetic' in the sense that you attract certain forces. . . . "

"I suppose," Professor Leacock muttered darkly.

"Or," I rashly continued, "it might have been a more personal comment."

"Having to do with my person?" Professor Leacock shot back.

"In a sense, yes, your personal vastness that is, the entire entirety of your being one enters into as though it were a universe of its own, the way for example I myself, to choose a poor example, landed unknowingly in the Leacockian cosmos after that first fateful slip—"

"What are you getting at?" Leacock demanded. "Say what you *mean*."

"I meant, no, I don't think I meant anything at all, sir."

"If you don't *mean* anything, don't *say* anything," Leacock ordered. Then he gave me one of his famous mock-fierce stares, the way he often did when he was joking, but this time I realized that he was angry and disappointed.

He saw me standing on the platform. Immediately he stood up, opened the window and called my name. Before I could reply he had withdrawn, only to reappear seconds later, my suitcase in his hand. As it dropped towards the con-crete platform, the train whistle gave its piercing shriek—yet in the midst of that deafening farewell I was sure I could hear Professor Leacock murmuring, "Chk. Chk."

"Chk. Chk," I replied and we raised our hands to each other as the train filed into the sunset.

Thus ended my years as private secretary to Stephen Leacock, the famed Canadian humorist.

napoleon
in moscow

1

NAPOLEON IS DEAD and everyone wants to know: How did it happen? Was it death by poison, from the boredom of exile, the heartbreak of a last absurd campaign to build a last futile empire? Napoleon is dead, but I prefer to remember Napoleon in his days of glory, Napoleon at his most mysterious. Napoleon in Moscow.

We are in the square outside his winter palace. Stella's excited breath tickling my ear as she clutches my arm and we kick our booted feet in the thick snow. Above us, Napoleon's window, heavy with golden candlelight, glows into the dark night.

While the moon recovers from last night's eclipse, snow falls hard from the sullen sky, and otters lie dreaming in their riverbank homes. On the lonely road that passes by my cabin, a snowplough moans; its blue revolving light flashes through my window and across the room.

Snow swirls and beats against the window. I am Napoleon in Moscow. My soldiers occupy the squares and swarm through the twisted streets in search of food. Nothing will be safe from me.

I am listening to Japanese music. I am trying to make sense of my life. My plan is to get the life problem structured, then carry on the way I used to, your normal greedy, selfish, manic-depressive person.

What I'm looking for now is a new master plan. I always used to have goals. For example, when I was a real estate salesman, which in a half-hearted way I still am, my goal first expressed itself in the number of houses I sold. After a while I dropped the pretence and it was just a matter of making a certain amount of money. Excuses: wife, children, mortgage, etc. I'm not talking anything fancy.

The old life was Stella. The children. The nights we spent trying to make the numbers balance. Afterwards, but not always, we would go upstairs and balance on each other. Even on nights like this, with the snow falling heavy and the revolving blue light of the snowplough like a searchlight sweeping our white bellies.

I am Napoleon in Moscow. "Napoleon in Moscow!" Stella laughed. This was after she had left, not necessarily forever, just a "trial separation" as she said, a holiday during which she would take the children and stay in town with her sister whose house was too big anyway—guess who sold it to her!—and since then, to tell the truth, the trial has been dragging on.

"That's me," I said, "Napoleon in Moscow."

"How do you know?"

"Demons called me on the telephone. I thought it was some kind of police association lottery. But they insisted.

The next morning I found the word 'Napoleon' tattooed on my left palm."

"I think you're letting yourself go," Stella said.

As Napoleon I faced a different configuration. I could lie on Stella and use her body to trace out my campaigns. But the truth is that despite his reputation, Napoleon was more interested in snow. That is why he had his men die there, rather than while making love with their loved ones.

2

My deeds will be recorded. Museums will rise in my name. The earth will be torn apart, shovels and pickaxes wielded in a chorus louder than any marching band to extract the lead from which millions of toy soldiers will be made in my image. Small boys the world over will turn me in their fingers. They will marvel at the splendour of my uniform, the bizarre cannonball shape of my head, the way I keep one hand warm by holding it inside my jacket. "Napoleon," those young voices will whisper in the night. The way my soldiers have always whispered my name. In the night. Full of admiration, dread and wonder. Why does he do it? they ask themselves. Who is it winds up this tiny conquest machine? With what light burns that brain which keeps inventing ways to raise and then exhaust armies on the world's battlefields? Etc.

The truth is, I have no answers. First I created the Empire, then the Empire created me. World history is a ping-pong match between my inscrutable unstoppable self and the marvels that self has created. And I? The *moi* behind the mask? Just another orphan soul tossing on the seas of destiny, even though those seas move to the tides I myself have caused.

The truth is that like all great French generals and statesmen, I am a man of action by default. My real vocation was to be a writer but my early stories were rejected by corrupt monarchist editors who wished to suppress the truth about Corsica. Before they went to the blade, my poems were taped to their mouths. Now I feel most myself in the night silence of my tent, the candles sputtering, the white paper stretching out in creamy reams softer than the eyeball of an empress. My letters to Josephine, my diaries of war, but most of all the words unwritten, the vast armies of prose I would send marching across untold pages —those unwritten armies that have sunk into the whiteness of paper like my troops into the snow of the endless Russian plains.

Lost, yes, because words cannot equal the splendour of these pre-dawn hours, the wonder of being alone in a tent near tomorrow's battlefield. Outside my canvas the starry sky sparkles over the heads of my sleeping troops, four hundred thousand men lurching towards the dawn, towards the first light that will jerk them awake, full of fear and hunger and that wild chaos only I can harness, only I can turn into an orderly hurricane of violence that will send them flying into the enemy, hacking and being hacked until their skins split, their bones shatter, their blood masses in stinking pools slowly draining to dark patches on the earth so at the end of the day, as the sun sets on the dead and the dying, as the cries of the wounded rise above the surgeons' saws and the hasty whispered prayers of my priests, I, Napoleon, repulsed, sated, sick at heart, fulfilled, I will mourn that great unconscious mass of men who sleep around me now; I will mourn their dead and crippled horses, their orphans, the rivers of wine they will never drink, the aging flesh their hands will never know. Monster, yes, that is the title with which history will reward me, but I am most at home in my lonely simple tent, doing the job that has been left to me, the manufacture of dreams and nightmares, sending my word-rich armies onto their pages of snow, letting them cancel and slaughter each other until all that remains is a brief and elegant poem, a few nostalgic blood-tinted lines limping towards eternity, yes, that's how I want to be re-membered, bleeding and limping in rags across the snow, or even forget the blood, the rags, the snow, the limp. Just me.

3

When the blackness of night expands blue and yellow, I step outside and strap on my skis. At this hour snow creaks. Branches snap. My troops stir amongst the leafless ghostly poplars that rise with the sun from the snow, arch their frozen branches into the cold liquid light pouring up from the eastern horizon. A few strides and the cabin is behind me, the pale hint of a lantern, a whiff of woodsmoke, then nothing at all as I glide into the soft belly of my marsh, coast down into the dark piny bush that waits to embrace me.

4

My bucking Bronco bucks and bronks. My two-hundred-and-eighty-six-horse cavalry moans, then roars and whin-nies beneath the snow-covered hood, white stuff flies in all directions as we power our way towards the road, leaving behind us the great rutted tracks of our charge.

The empire of the sun is back. Its weak light shines through veils of swirling snow, low half-convinced clouds that lie crouched along the horizon. The black asphalt of the highway has been scraped clean. The school buses have already passed to pick up their roadside cargoes of ski-jacketed children. Now all that remains in front of each house is its pile of lopsided green garbage bags and blue recycling boxes, waiting for the yellow township trucks.

On the way to my office I pass the dump. Despite last night's snow, the air is still and clearing. They're having a little burn-off; smoke raises straight and orderly towards the washed-out dome of the sky. The dump is where I open my thermos. I love the way the steam rises into my face, the bittersweet coffee scalds my waiting tongue.

Twenty minutes later and I'm at my office, a cube in a plaza off the main highway. Frank has been and gone. The office smells of baseboard heaters, wet wool, prehistoric pizza crusts. When the red light starts blinking I pick up the phone. It's Stella, unusually.

"You all right?"

"Of course."

"Frank said . . ."

"Frank called you?"

"Last night, of course, after. . ."

Last night after work Frank and I went to Aunt Lucy's, grabbed something to eat in the sports bar. Frank is always going for the nachos, pure grease, but even if it is crazy to worry about vegetables I like a plate of crunchies with the cheese dip. Then a hamburger. Not exactly a health spa special but at least the kind of meal you could admit to

your doctor. A few beers and maybe this is crazy but after
a certain number it's not that good for you so I switch to
Scotch and water. At least you know what you're getting
and where you are.

Last night after the switch I told Frank, nothing intended,
that his face was starting to look like the nachos he was eating, tomato red with yellow stuff bubbling around the edges.
"Look at your nose," I now remembered saying, Stella's silence bringing it all back, "one big glob of pepperoni."

"I didn't mean to hurt his feelings," I told Stella.

"He fired you," Stella said.

We'd been yelling in the parking lot and then Frank had
screamed something about my not coming back. I'd picked
him up by the coat, not really meaning to hurt him. That
was when he'd let me have it in the face. Wouldn't have
thought he could. Left me there with my nose spouting like
a hydrant.

"Wanted me to call and apologize for him. Ask you to
come back."

"Here I am."

"Well, I'm here," Stella said.

"The kids at school?"

"That's right."

A questioning silence settled in. Stella's sister was in
Florida. The kids were gone for hours. My nose was fine
and I had my job back. "You hoping for a visit?"

"*Hoping?*" Stella repeated, giving the word a half twist
and just enough vinegar to let me know she could have
drowned it if she wanted to.

I put my hand in my jacket. I'd lost the opening skir-
mish, but as every general knows, you can't win a battle
unless you manage to engage the enemy.

"Well," I said, sounding a note of defeat and withdrawal.

"I'm out of coffee," Stella said. "You could pick some up on the way."

It is easier to conquer a country than a heart. Napoleon said that. Or perhaps it was me. It's amazing what I can come out with, mostly by accident, when I've had an extra cup of coffee or a few glasses of Scotch and a few thousand brain cells are tipped into mass suicide. Stella of course, Stella doesn't appreciate these little dictums. She doesn't want to play Josephine to my Napoleon. "Well, then, you can be my Stella," I once offered her, but she didn't realize what I meant, she never takes the long view, Stella, the backward glance from the future that allows us to know that what we're going through is just so much history waiting to be corrected by a little make-up, various lies and omissions, various inventions pointless to try to guess in advance. She thinks, to put it bluntly, that what's happening right now is some kind of "reality." I do my best to adjust, pretend, sometimes even try to convince myself, but in the end I'm back to the long view, the realization Stella is but one of a number of campaigns, a point, perhaps even the high point, of my life-to-be with her as-yet-unencountered successors. "Stella," I'll one day sigh, possibly with the same bitter regret and loss I often feel for her even now. She'll have forgotten me. She'll be in some new present, some new "reality." Her life with me will be summed up by a few pictures in an album and the odd memory that catches her unexpectedly in the ribs.

We start off in the kitchen. To show goodwill I myself put the water in the kettle, though my hands begin to tremble and it spills before I can even get it to the stove. "You might as well come upstairs," Stella then says, not unkindly.

I follow her up. She's wearing a soft white sweater of wool so fine I can't imagine it between my fingers, dark pants stretched tight over the bum I also want to touch. While I sit on the edge of her sister's bed Stella goes into the bathroom to undress, then comes back in her white terry-cloth robe, the one I bought her last Christmas.

We climb in. In the morning winter light our skin is grainy, helpless. Soon we're under the sheets, humping and groaning. Do we love each other or are we just condemned to this weird sweet need? Afterwards we're lying side by side, and I'm looking up at my sister-in-law's pink stuccoed ceiling wondering if she too has inspected this dubious touch in the afterglow of sex, and then the whole need comes on us again. This time, hovering above Stella, I open my eyes and look down on her. Her white legs are spread in a perfect V, and I suddenly remember when Crystal was born: just before the final contractions Stella was lying this way, her legs splayed, exhausted, then suddenly her knees jerked up, her face and throat turned scarlet, her huge belly banded with muscle and effort—

In the shower my nose starts to bleed again, though not as badly as when Frank hit me. To save the towels I stand above the sink, holding toilet paper to my face. When I come back into the bedroom Stella is lying where I left her, hands clasped behind her head, making her own study of the pink stucco.

"You could stay for supper," Stella says.

I want to see the children. I want Stella. I want to slip into this pink stucco cocoon and sleep away my life until I come out dead on the other side.

But there's something in this I can't do. I can't burden the brightness of their living with the awkward shadow of my death, of my long view in which after all the dazzling campaigns, the retreats, the exiles, the empires constructed out of countries not yet named, the years spent in dungeons not yet built, I'll be lying in the ground somewhere and they'll be standing over me, not sure whether to weep or just be relieved.

"Don't make it into a big thing," Stella says.

I sit down on the edge of the bed. Outside the snow is sheeting against the windows. "Look at it," I say.

Stella pulls the sheets and covers up to her neck. "At least you could bring me some of the coffee you promised."

"I also got some wine."

"The corkscrew's in the drawer beside the fridge."

Soon all the windows are plastered with snow. We're plastered too, not really, just dizzy with all the times we keep going back to Stella's sister's bed. By the time we make it down to the kitchen, more or less dressed, to find something to eat, it's mid-afternoon and according to the radio, the highways and the schools are closing.

When school lets out we're both there. Crystal and Robbie have their scarves wrapped round their faces, the snow is blowing into everyone's eyes, we stagger into my bucking Bronco and drive the few blocks home without anyone doing anything but clapping their hands and panting.

I help Crystal, who is seven, out of her snowpants. She looks at me curiously at first, it's been weeks, then just goes along as though everything is normal, as though I've been here every night for the past several months kissing her beet-red cheeks, helping her in and out of clothes, reading her stories while she waits for her bath. Robbie, five, stays in the circle of his mother's arms, watching suspiciously. But when I pick him up he throws his arms around my neck and presses his face into my chest so hard that it hurts.

When all the coats and boots are piled up they run off to the family room I was so careful to point out to Carrie when she bought the house. Sprawled out on the apricot shag wall-to-wall that was featured in the ad, they watch the big colour television Carrie's husband Cal bought for the Stanley Cup a few years ago. Stella and I can see them from the kitchen. While she makes hot chocolate I look in the freezer and cupboards. "I'll do spaghetti," I announce, as though about to distribute a cordon bleu meal to my troops stranded knee-deep on the Russian steppes.

"Great," Stella says. "A night off cooking. That calls for another bottle of wine."

The house I sold Carrie is warm. There's real central heating, a gas furnace that blasts hot air through the house with Desert Storm efficiency, along with a living-room gas fireplace the designer built in as part of the guaranteed romance such a palace inspires. While I hack away at the onions, Stella opens a new bottle, turns on the fireplace so the flames start making their gassy blue dance. The living-room carpet isn't shag, just a dark broadloom meant to hide the dirt. The ceiling is stucco, like the ones in the bedrooms upstairs and the family room, but since we're downstairs it's not pink but white. I wonder what it would be like to lie here, naked, in front of the romantic fireplace, looking up at the white stucco. Stella has already poured the wine. If the kids weren't here, I think to myself, we could try it right now. But of course the kids are here, because we tried it right now before, and so—etc., etc. Anyway, what kind of father am I, wanting my own children whom I don't really take care of to disappear so I can make more neglected children?

Stella now has on the kind of slacks women wear these days, wide hips, narrow little cuffs that hug their tiny ankles. One of those tiny ankles is crossed over her knee. She's sitting on one of the two matching white corduroy couches, reading a psychology textbook. That book, the master's degree program it's part of, was one of the reasons Stella gave for moving to town. It's basic to her plan, her master master's plan, at the end of which she'll have her own cube, not in a doughnut plaza off the highway but in a tastefully renovated downtown house, in which she'll "help women help themselves." She won't bother helping men help themselves, it goes without saying, because they already have, pigs at the trough, and if now they're sad and confused, well, it's just like a kid who steals too many candies and then gets sick from eating too much. Or is disappointed because they stop tasting sweet. Or angry that the people he robbed no longer like him.

While Stella reads her psychology text I dive into one of Carrie's magazines. It falls open to an article on composting vegetables. Almost every line is highlighted. I wish I could ask her how a person who lives in a house with stucco ceilings could spend her life composting vegetables but first of all she only lives in this house because she bought it to please Stella and second I've already asked her this kind of question and she doesn't even try to answer.

I switch to coffee and by the time I'm laying the steaming plates of spaghetti out on the table, I'm stone sober. Stella, meanwhile, has flaked out on one of the white corduroy sofas. I find her lying on her back, one leg hooked over the back of the sofa, one hand flung out to the coffee table, still wrapped around her wine glass. Her cheeks are flushed, her face in unusual and angelic repose. Feeling like

Santa Claus I rearrange her a bit and cover her with one of Carrie's fuzzy angora blankets.

During dinner I quiz the children about life in their new school. As though I am some interested relative who just dropped in from Mars, not the unstable father because of whom their mother had to move the children out of their natural home and into this new school where they had to make all new friends and get used to different teachers.

Afterwards they show me their new room. Their pink stucco. They sleep in twin wood-framed beds that can be stacked to make bunks. On their beds are their favourite quilts, their stuffed toys, a few picture books I recognize. When I sit down on Crystal's bed she immediately snuggles up to me, demands that I read her a story about a brave worm, one I've read to her a thousand times before. Robbie pretends to be above all this. But he stretches out on his own bed and listens as I read.

One at a time I get them into their pyjamas, teeth and hair brushed, faces washed, the whole routine. Wind and snow are still rattling the windows. It is so warm here, so whole. I imagine the cabin, half-frozen and dark. As always, when I'm not there for the night, I feel uncomfortably disloyal, as though I've deserted my post.

When the children are ready I take them downstairs to kiss their mother good night. Stella is awake again, sipping a cup of coffee and reading in front of the fire. The children crowd around her. She draws them under the blanket. Soon they're chattering away, animated and oblivious.

That night we go to bed together as though I'd never left. So strange-familiar, Stella's body next to mine. This time when we make love it's like animals opening to each other in their cave. Stella falls asleep, holding me. When

I wake up, she's still wrapped around my back. I listen to the snow and wind. There are night lights in the hall and bathroom for the children, and when I close my eyes I can imagine those lights glowing outside, in the storm. My future self—or one of Stella's lovers—could be standing on the street, seeing the glow of these lights, speculating on the mystery behind the windows.

For hours I lie there, imagining myself being imagined. I am trying to believe I am really real, really here, really asleep in Stella's arms. But every time I close my eyes I float up above the house. First I see us, yes, the happy family happily ensconced in our gas-powered central-heated warmth. But then I go higher; the whole town is just a red-yellow smear of lights, and I am floating north, up the frozen ribbons of highway and then into the back country thick with scrub and beaver ponds. Until I come to the cabin, stranded and battered by snow, deserted by the only one who can love and watch over it.

5

In the morning I leave early, as the children are preparing for school. The snowploughs have passed in the night, my bucking Bronco has no problem blasting its way out of the driveway and into the street. I go to a restaurant for bacon and eggs, double brown toast no butter, a newspaper and endless coffee until my nerves set up a high whining chatter.

When I arrive at the office Frank immediately starts talking about the Redway deal we've been working on for months—a strip plaza location for which we levered the land, fought for all the clearances and permits, and are now trying to unload in order to fill our bank accounts. Or at least pay our rent. Or something. It's so long since we've made a deal I can hardly remember the name of our lawyer.

This morning Frank is full of optimism. He's got on his lucky blue selling jacket, his face is shaved so close he looks like he's had his skin peeled. The blueprints are spread out on his desk and, this is how good Frank is, once he gets talking even I believe I can smell the fresh doughnuts and coffee from the little shop he's got marked out on the corner.

We're meeting the potential buyers in a downtown restaurant at noon, and just as we're getting ready to leave, Stella calls. Frank, giving me a big wink as though I'm about to pop the question, passes me the phone. I've just come out from our little washroom, my own face scraped raw by one of those disposable razors that you keep using for one more shave.

"How are you?" she asks.

"Nervous," I say. "We're trying to unload the plaza this morning."

Frank frowns. He doesn't like negative remarks except when he's into the nachos and beer.

"Good luck," Stella says, her voice empty. Of course she wasn't calling to ask about what I was or wasn't selling.

"I'll let you know how it goes later," I say, evading everything, leaving everything open. This is, as I often lecture my troops, known as taking possession of the high ground.

Stella responds with a direct and immediate attack. "Later?"

This is what it is to be Napoleon. This is what it is.

"I'll call you from the cabin," I concede, digging my own grave.

6

When I get home the snow is red with the setting sun. I go straight to the woodpile and let my splitting axe say it all, its huge iron head rearing back in the darkness, then descending into the frozen wood with a loud mourning shriek.

Later that night I am out in the snow. The bucking Bronco is a dark outline in the moonlight, my own windows cast their golden glow like abandoned tears. As my skis scream softly on the frozen snow I am free to imagine that behind those gold-lit windows Napoleon is gathering his forces, charting out his marches, planning the conquests of new far-flung empires, vast frozen hearts.

I move towards the pine woods. Thorns tear at my legs and face. Until finally I am safe in the darkness, dying to the shrill cries of winter owls, slivers of moonlight feasting on my blood.

playing
dead

AARON MET MICHELLE on his first trip to Paris. That was before Rose. Or *Rhuz* as Michelle called her, with a peculiar lack of emphasis as though to point out that in French this word was mostly either an adjective or a way of cooking meat—certainly not a word that could aspire to the status of a proper noun, let alone an actual person.

That winter Aaron's official reason for being in Paris had been to research the "secular feminism of Simone de Beauvoir," a thesis topic with a scientific basis: he had invented it with the aid of chemicals. Unfortunately it dissolved when exposed to the social whirl of a group of New Yorkers who were paying for the romance of Paris by providing the English subtitles for under-the-counter videos.

Michelle was dating one of those men. He was not originally from New York but Buenos Aires, and he claimed to have been a professional tennis player before he tore his rotator cuff and had to go into opera singing. Michelle was undergoing psychoanalysis as part of her training to become an analyst herself. Her hair was jet black and fell to her shoulders, her eyes were full of sympathy and her mouth twitched constantly with the hidden meanings of things—

hidden meanings she and Aaron would joke about as the group made its late-night perambulations around the Latin Quarter or gathered for drinks in the spectacular apartment Michelle had inherited after the tragic death of a childless uncle in an airplane crash.

"My brother," Michelle would sometimes call Aaron, as they walked arm in arm. Michelle was the youngest of six sisters and therefore had, her analysis revealed, a large uncompensated curiosity about men. She moved forward in a slow swaying stroll that was a mixture of trying to get somewhere and, on the other hand, standing still and shifting her hips back and forth as though she were at the edge of a dance floor.

Like Michelle, Aaron had large eyes and dark hair. By the time he met Michelle, his dark hair ended in cleanly trimmed sideburns. But years before, when he was still a boy, the black hair of his sideburns grew down from his temples in long wispy curls that followed the curves of his ears. Even after he started shaving, the pale narrow islet between ear and beard shadow reminded Aaron of his adolescent self. He would see it in memory and also, strangely, in photographs of ghetto children. Not that he sought them out: but there were times when just leafing though a magazine could confront him with one of these pictures of young adolescents, nameless clones whose ghastly deaths could not be counterbalanced by the fact that their genes had reappeared in an unjustly safe North American boy called Aaron Fine, a boy who couldn't figure out how to mourn the absence of his vanished doubles.

If Aaron had one strength, he would say to himself (though he would also admit that perhaps he didn't), it was his constant awareness of that absence—call that absence racial guilt, the existential abyss, the desire for an impossible third piece of toast. If he had one weakness (though he would also admit he had many), it was his eagerness to take seriously anyone or anything that appeared to fill the absence, however temporarily.

Sometimes, when he had drunk more than he should, he would wonder if the missing piece of himself might turn out to be Michelle. But that first winter Michelle had her tennis player/opera singer and then whenever Aaron returned to Paris there was someone else, a continually exploding galaxy of artists, intellectuals, businessmen with odd businesses.

Then Rose arrived. For some reason their relationship immediately struck him as vaguely illegal because his grandmother had also been called Rose.

After Rose, Aaron forgot to send Michelle his annual Christmas card and then, even worse, he took three weeks to return a phone call because, although he concealed this from Michelle, Rose had written the message on the back of a cleaning stub.

"She'll probably refuse to see me," Aaron complained, packing for what would be his first trip to Paris in two years. Since meeting Michelle he had graduated from having drinks with people who wrote subtitles to making short television documentaries and working for a production company with a small set of offices but large ambitions.

"Send her flowers," Rose said.

Shortly after Aaron arrived in Paris he telephoned Michelle. After two rings her answering machine came on, beginning with a brief silence, which Aaron always thought was Michelle's way of reminding callers that she was a psychoanalyst and that her voice was issuing forth from a deep tomb of professional certainty. Michelle's message was: "Please leave your name and number." Aaron had several times observed Michelle as she sat watching the answering machine, her face transformed into that of a predatory feline as she listened to her unhelpful message along with the stammered words that followed.

The telephone was not in the living room itself, but in what Michelle called the doll room. It was a small glass-shelved alcove, with neither window nor door, that would have been ideal for a comfortable sofa and reading lamp. On the shelves were rows of dolls along with various metal and ceramic holders for candles and incense. The floor was covered by a thick oriental rug and piled with satin cushions. In a corner, arranged on a small dark pine pedestal, was the telephone and its answering machine. Aaron supposed this room—candles ablaze, incense smoking, dolls' shadows flickering like a silent chorus of goddesses—must be where Michelle seduced the men she was always talking about.

One night early in their friendship, when its boundaries were still unknown, Michelle invited him into the apartment after one of their post-dinner strolls, turned out all the lights and lit the candles in the doll room. But when Michelle's hand stretched towards him it was only to give him a bottle of wine and an opener. Then she settled herself into some cushions and explained that she'd had the dolls ever since she was a child, and that even then she'd had a special place for them: the floor of her cupboard. She would, she said, shut herself inside, light a candle and play concentration camp.

"I don't know that game," Aaron said.

"It was very hard for the dolls. Often they would disobey and would have to be punished or beaten. But in the end I always forgave them. I would leave them with little pieces of candy or sugar lumps in their mouths. The next day the treats would be gone. I would ask them how they had tasted and sometimes at first I believed they were eating them."

"And then?"

"At night I could hear the mice in my cupboard fighting over the sweets. Soon the sweets weren't enough. The mice were very greedy and they began eating at the faces of my dolls. In the mornings there would be toothmarks on their lips and cheeks. Some of the dolls needed operations which I did with a knife and some plaster. I told them it was their own fault for being such messy eaters but now I always feel bad when I think of the mice chewing on their faces. You know—"

Which was when the telephone started to ring. A soft trilling that emanated from its pine pedestal, and was repeated from the office down the hall and the kitchen. Aaron had never been in Michelle's bedroom but he supposed she had a telephone there, too. The answering machine finally clicked on, followed by Michelle's message.

"*Santé*," said Michelle, raising her glass. "Don't make faces over my dolls. They had a hard childhood but now, because I feel so bad, they have a passion for life. Look how happy they are. All day they play dead, then I come and keep them company."

"They sit and listen to the telephone ring."

"Yes, but they must never answer."

"Just like you."

Michelle raised her hand to correct him. "I am the doll *maîtresse*. I am permitted to answer if I want but if I answer too often I lose my power."

The phone began to ring again. "That will be Ivan. Some nights he calls me every fifteen minutes. I have nothing to say to him so I just—"

"Play dead."

"Exactly. You see? I have taught you something."

"Do I get a piece of sugar?"

"For you, a chocolate." Michelle burst into laughter and refilled their glasses. "Don't forget to wash your face before you go to sleep."

"Aaron Fine," Aaron said. "I'm in Paris for ten days. Let's have dinner if you're free." Then he left his phone number along with the information that he had no answering machine in the apartment he was subletting.

"How do you get rid of all these men you always talk about?" he had once asked her.

"When they telephone? As I showed you. I play dead."

"Even if they come to the door?"

"Same thing. I don't answer. I play dead."

They always spoke in French and as Aaron's French was defective at best, he was often uncertain if he had understood her correctly. His speech was even worse than his comprehension. Every now and then he would get off two or three sentences so amazingly perfect that even he knew what he had said. "That was good," he would congratulate himself, then relapse into his usual slurred garble. No one seemed to mind. "How can you bear it?" he once asked Michelle. "Even I can't understand myself."

"That's your charm," she said. And added: "Everyone makes a few mistakes. Don't be a baby."

The evening after Aaron left his message for Michelle, his telephone rang. "Jean-Louis?" a woman's voice enquired.

The voice was so like Michelle's in all its different textures that for a moment Aaron thought she was playing a game with him. "Jean-Louis?" the woman asked again, and this time there was a note of doubt. In the course of explaining that she had the wrong number, Aaron made a grammatical mistake so ridiculous that even he started to giggle, and the woman responded with a laugh that swept away all the wanting and uncertainty and expectation in such a spontaneous burst that Aaron laughed with her. About half an hour later she called again; this time Aaron had one of his flashes of competence and managed to explain that Jean-Louis's absence from this particular telephone was permanent. Sober-voiced and guarded, the woman thanked him and hung up.

Afterwards Aaron thought about how, if he were in a movie, the spontaneous laugh would have turned into an encounter, the encounter into a romance, the romance into a comedy.

In fact that was how he had met Rose: in a movie. A French movie, *The Discreet Charm of the Bourgeoisie*, which had been showing at a Toronto art cinema where Aaron had gone alone, wearing his snappiest leather jacket for protection, only to find himself sitting beside a young woman howling with such glee that her popcorn literally flew out of its bag and began to shower Aaron. Aaron, too sophisticated to laugh aloud at images he'd seen a dozen times, found himself brushing at his jacket and wishing this ill-behaved neighbour had skipped the salt and butter. Afterwards, standing in the lobby and still trying to clean his jacket, he thought how this incident had proven, if proof were needed, how pointless it was for an unattached male such as himself to seek consolation in clothes. "Sorry," Rose said to Aaron, her voice coming from behind and surprising him. Her girlfriend had conveniently disappeared.

"It's okay," Aaron said grumpily. "At least you were too cheap to buy a drink."

"I could give you my lawyer's phone number so you could sue me." Rose raised her eyebrows as if daring Aaron—or was it inviting him?

"I'll settle for a drink," Aaron said, although of course he didn't.

As for the unnamed woman in search of Jean-Louis—it was easy for Aaron to see they were not in the same movie. Standing reflectively in his apartment and contemplating their destinies, Aaron was in a movie about his trip to Paris and his bad French. The unnamed woman wasn't worried about her French. She *was* French. And she was in a movie with the mysterious Jean-Louis. Her role was the one most French women past adolescence were compelled to play. The role of the beautiful woman whose perfect teenage blankness—the cultivated Lolita-esque indifference that once made her so attractive to men—is gradually being overwritten by neurosis, intelligence, sensitivity and the knowledge that instead of being exciting and adventurous, most French men would rather worry about their jobs.

In the unnamed woman's voice Aaron had heard a lifetime of pent-up desire for a better world. Along with all the anxiety, insecurity and frustration that could only result from realizing fate had sentenced her to life as a Frenchwoman. She had released all these feelings, and more, in searching out this mysterious Jean-Louis who had not even deigned to give her his correct number. He was obviously someone she knew only by his first name—she had tried him twice—and now she was going to have to think about whether or why he had deliberately misled her.

In the movie, Aaron knew, she would take a few steps away from the phone and look down at the match cover where he had written his number. Perhaps there would be a flash to the bar or bedroom where the actual deed had taken place.

Jean-Louis was, it suddenly struck Aaron, playing dead in his own way. But instead of making his victim record her desperate voice on his answering machine, he preferred to pass her on to a stranger.

The next day Aaron woke up late and with a headache. He drank a double espresso at a café while examining his map to find the way to the Picasso Museum. The museum was in the Marais, and as Aaron approached it he reflected on the meaning of the French word, swamp, and on the fact that swamped was how he always felt in Paris—swamped, overwhelmed, drawn down into a murky fecund world where unknown forces wrapped their tentacles around him and sucked him into their weird bubbly root systems filled with bizarre snails and eels and catfish all fastening onto him with their round vampire teeth, and sucking out his fluids until his consciousness finally began to melt into the dark primal French ooze.

In the museum, the exhibits were chronologically ordered. He could see Picasso had gone through the same process—his early brilliantly stylish paintings with their airy lines first breaking into cubes, then dissolving into smear as the decades took their toll. While part of Aaron's mind elaborated this theory of the destruction of Picasso's eye and talent, another portion eavesdropped on the conversations around him. If Michelle had been there, with her fluent Spanish and German, she could have supplied the strands of those languages in exchange for what he was hearing with perfect clarity: the heated complaints of a British couple convinced it was impossible to buy hot chocolate in Paris.

Aaron almost said to them, "Why don't you shut up and go home? Or try any bar or restaurant?" Instead he began to feel conspicuously alone, and left.

That evening he went out with a friend from the old circle. They ended up at a restaurant owned by the woman who would have been his friend's sister-in-law had his friend not broken the engagement by producing a doctor's certificate attesting that he was an alcoholic.

The next morning, when the telephone rang, it was Rose asking how his work was going. Aaron was supposed to be researching a documentary on a Canadian historian who had lived in Paris during the thirties. But the strangely seeking phone call from the woman who had been betrayed by Jean-Louis had inspired Aaron in other directions. "I went out with Stéphane last night and now I have a hangover."

"Stéphane always gives you a hangover."

"I tried calling Michelle."

"She likes you," Rose said.

"She hasn't called me back."

"Send her flowers."

Rose told him that two feet of snow had fallen in Toronto and that the subway had stopped working. Aaron looked guiltily out the window as she described the fire escape at the back of their apartment, now thigh-deep in snow. "It's like Finland here," she said.

The wall opposite his courtyard window was a dazzling white he'd learned was the signal that a cloudless blue sky was awaiting him. When he got downstairs the first thing he did was buy a newspaper. It contained a travel supplement, and while having his double espresso at the corner café, Aaron began leafing through it. Coincidentally there was a feature on the northern regions of Finland. Residents boasted that if trapped outside in the cold they could—at will—lower their body temperature to survive.

"It's a trick we learned at school," one man explained proudly. His wife added that all Finns were also able to make fires by rubbing sticks together.

Aaron wished he could ask this couple, right now, what stopped their bodies from freezing when they lowered their temperatures to seventy below zero. Of course he knew this was a stupid question. Millions of Finns had probably spent whole generations at seventy below, but he was still curious. Then he found himself imagining, instead of a newspaper travel supplement, a newspaper love supplement in which Michelle explained how she did almost the same thing—lowered her emotional temperature and rubbed electronic waves together in order to make the telephone ring—a trick every Frenchwoman had learned to perform in school. When the phone rang her now hibernating heart could listen with absolute serenity.

When he got home from an afternoon wasted at the National Archives, Aaron called Michelle again. She answered on the first ring. "Oui." Her voice was in the flatline mode she used when picking up during an analytic session.

"It's Aaron," Aaron said. "I was in Paris and I thought I would call you."

"I got your message."

Aaron pictured Michelle in her doctor's chair, a giant

leather throne that towered over the velvet-covered ré-
camier on which her patients divulged themselves.

"Well, then," Aaron said, "goodbye."

"We'll talk on Thursday." But she didn't hang up.

"Are you with a patient?"

"Yes."

"A man or a woman?"

"You must know these things."

"I think you're giving erotic therapy." He had wanted to
say "lessons in group sex," but hadn't known how to say
"group sex" in French. It was inconceivable he would have
said such a thing in English. Once in a restaurant, when he
had accidentally spilled a glass of water, Michelle explained
to the people seated beside him that he was a British psychopath who had been sent to France to have a lobotomy
under her supervision. It turned out that both members of
the couple were architects, and that one of their close
friends had needed to undergo electroshock treatments.
There was a long discussion about which procedure would
be best for Aaron. In the end they decided on lobotomy,
and the wife drew, on Aaron's skull, the paths which the
surgeons' knives and drills should follow. She claimed that
before going to architecture school she had worked for a
Paris designer, drawing clothes on to the skin of models.
Had Aaron not been cast in the role of a British psychopath,
he would have explained that in Canada such occupations
were almost unknown, and that the vast majority of the
population were either some form of middle manager or
unemployed.

Michelle didn't respond to the "erotic therapy" ploy.
Instead she said she would call him back. "Au revoir," she
ended.

"Au revoir," Aaron repeated. He knew he had triumphed, or at least been forgiven, because the last time she had spoken she had ended with a dramatic "Adieu," which he presumed meant that their relationship had been sent out into the snow to lower its temperature forever.

"You're crazy," Michelle said a few nights later. They were in one of those restaurants where the staff treated her as though she lived upstairs and brought them Christmas presents every week. "I thought we might not see each other for a long time. You have your family, I have my work."

"I always come to Paris. You know that."

Michelle looked down at her glass. Over the years her face had evolved from oval to round. But her eyes still flickered with her ten thousand plans, just as her lips still constantly twitched as though it was only a question of when and where she would pounce. Her hair, soft and dark, was shorter now: instead of coming down to her shoulders it curved around her cheeks to her neck.

"I was about to get married," Michelle said. "A German —very nice, very cultivated, very rich. The problem was that I didn't want to give up my apartment. And you know it's too small for two. He was very understanding. He said I could lease it to someone for a year or two. To be sure. Or simply keep it and use it as my office while I lived with him."

"What a man," Aaron said. He couldn't believe the jealous tone of his own voice.

"He knew how to make me happy in certain ways," Michelle said.

"Please."

"And an excellent cook. When he would come here, he always called the chef out to get the recipe."

Aaron could just see them, sitting around the house bottle of cognac, the chef leaning back in his bloodstained apron explaining the fine points of the rabbit civet that seemed to be the house specialty.

"Thanks for bringing me to this historic site. Why didn't you marry him?"

"I did. Not at city hall, of course. But I said let's pretend we're married and go on a honeymoon. If it works out, I will introduce you to my mother."

"Too bad it didn't."

"But it did. Our honeymoon was a great success. We went mountain climbing in the Swiss Alps."

Aaron summoned the French to ask if her lover wore leather shorts.

"You would have loved his legs. They were so big and hairy."

The worst thing about love, Rose had once told Aaron, was that afterwards you could no longer remember exactly how it felt. This announcement came only a few hours after she had offered him her lawyer's phone number, and Aaron found himself admiring the way this woman, at four o'clock in the morning and covered only by the sheet that was draped over their interlaced bodies, had the courage, or possibly the foresight, to dismiss in advance whatever might happen between them. It made his stomach hurt. The tone of her voice, cold and self-contained, sank into him and opened the old wound—which was how he always experienced the beginning of what other people called love and he thought of as a disease he was sometimes gripped by, an actual physical wound, the never-healed scar that separated the child he had once been from everything and everyone that child had so strongly desired and feared.

"Of course," Rose had said, "you probably make a profession of falling in love."

Aaron was sitting at the table in his rented Paris apartment. He had taken to carrying sheets of drawing paper and charcoal pencils when he travelled because now that the era of letters had ended, he had a new habit of having a last glass of wine late at night while sketching the faces of people he'd seen on the street. He thought of these drawings as a private vice: packing for the airport he would shred them into the wastebasket, and the pile of torn paper would always give him a feeling of great accomplishment.

But tonight it was Rose he wanted to draw. He gave her long charcoal-coloured hair, overly large round eyes, a slightly turned-up nose that was an inexplicable diminutive of what Rose called her matrician aspect, a mouth that came out right on the first try: a little too wide for her face, lips full and mobile, corners turned up as though to assure the world that this capable and sexy mouth belonged to a person of optimism tempered with irony, or possibly vice versa, which of course would be a whole different story.

Michelle's story was that while she and her trial husband were sitting on one of those mountain peaks her trial husband had forced her to climb, he had suffered some kind of heart attack, leather shorts and all. She had hammered his chest until his heart started again, then built a fire and fed him powdered mountain soup to give him the strength to continue. The episode had made her realize that the weight of destiny was equal to an apartment and, this very weekend, she told Aaron, she was going to Marseille to visit her mother and discuss the wedding plans.

"Who will be your best man?" Aaron asked, feeling ashamed, now that he knew the whole story, of feeling badly about eating at a restaurant where the man whose life Michelle had saved had gotten recipes from the chef.

"You, of course. Then I can meet the famous Rose." *Rhuz*, she still pronounced it, but with a little spark, as though after everything that had been revealed, this dubious word might be moving towards noun-status.

After his dinner with Michelle, Aaron stayed up half the night reading a book about Dostoyevsky searching St. Petersburg for his dead son.

In his dreams he confused himself with Dostoyevsky, Michelle with the son. But instead of playing with revolutionaries, Michelle played with the dolls she had once shown him. Even at the time, Aaron had thought they were ugly. Clumps of their hair had been torn out, and the wooden shoulders and arms were scarred, and there were places where the shellac had been chipped away. Despite Michelle's pride in her operations, many of the faces still looked chewed. There was one particularly disgusting doll with gouged toothmarks that ran in parallel trenches from the corner of one eye down to its paint-splashed lips.

In his dream he kept staring at that eye, until the doll's face around it turned into a grey-furred rat's face quivering with hunger and anticipation. He woke up to the sound of his own scream, rolling out of bed and hitting the pillow away. Even as he got up from the floor her was sure he could hear the scratch of the rodent's claws against the hardwood as it ran for cover.

Aaron was breathing hard and there was a grainy sweat

on his skin that reminded him of bad drugs. He stepped into the shower and stayed there until the hot water began to turn cold. As he dried himself it came to him that his dream hadn't been about himself at all, but was a signal that Michelle was in some kind of danger. He dialled her number, but after two rings the answering machine came on. He remembered then that Michelle had said she was going to see her mother about the wedding.

Three cups of strong coffee laid a pipeline of anxiety from his belly to his throat. He had an appointment to see an agent about arrangements to distribute his company's films, and by the time he'd had some bread and another cup of coffee all his worries were concentrated on the difficulties of breaking Canadian films into the French market.

The agent turned out to be a North African Jew who had spent ten years in Israel before emigrating to Paris. His name was Sol. He was tall and stylish in a cashmere jacket and closely tailored jeans. When he learned Aaron was Jewish he insisted on taking him to lunch at a restaurant in the Marais. Soon it was three o'clock in the afternoon and they were on their second bottle of wine. For the first time in days Aaron was totally relaxed. He leaned back in his chair as Sol, talking fast and constantly switching between English and French, wove his tale of strange intrigues in the Paris Jewish community. He spoke with such intense conviction that the existence of the external world—including the fact that Sol's agency had never managed to sell a single one of Aaron's company's films—was nothing more than a dubious shadow surrounding the small table between them. When they finally spilled out from the dark restaurant into the blinding afternoon light, Aaron found himself totally disoriented.

"Do you still have people to see here?" Sol asked as they were about to shake hands.

"Only my psychoanalyst," Aaron said, laughing.

"People still get psychoanalyzed? Who do you see?"

"She's just a friend. Michelle Carrière."

"Michelle—" Sol said, as though trying to remember something.

"Like the Beatles song. She's just a friend."

"A few years ago I went out with a psychoanalyst called Michelle. She had a beautiful apartment. She told me I would have to share her with her dolls."

Aaron watched Sol's face as it took on the expression that must have been intended to convey the nostalgia of past loves.

"And were you happy with her?" he finally asked, to end the conversation.

Sol shrugged his shoulders. "She wasn't my type. I was only trying to steal her from a friend."

That evening Aaron had planned to go to the movies. Instead he bought some American magazines and a take-out Chinese dinner. Reading about the lives of sports heroes and movie stars he felt soothed and finally so calm that on the pad of paper he'd intended for a script outline, he began a letter.

Dear Rose,
Although I have never written to you before, there is
much unsaid. Perhaps in this weighty unspoken lies the
success of our arrangement.

Aaron set his pen down. It made an interesting angle against the pad. He had never told Rose how or why he loved her but even though he was sitting at a capacious table, utterly calm and five thousand miles removed, he had no opinions on the subject. There was the bit about his grandmother. There were the insides of Rose's elbows, which for some reason he found particularly adorable.

> I have always admired your arms, especially the insides
> of your elbows. Also your perfectly shaped ears. I have
> even thought that the classic perfection of your ears
> must be a sign of some secret pact with the gods.

Aaron realized he would never send this letter because admitting to Rose that he knew she was in harmony with the gods would give her an advantage from which he could never recover. He crumpled the letter and began writing again, on a fresh sheet of paper:

> Dear Michelle,
> Although in the past I have found it easy to telephone
> you and, most of the time, easy to speak to your
> answering machine, when faced with a sheet of paper
> I discover that I have nothing left to say to you. Perhaps
> I have used up all my messages. Even the weight of the
> unspoken has entirely disappeared. I can only assume
> this means we are at last free of each other.

Aaron looked at the words he had written. Was this his reaction to Sol's story? What about his dream? And how could he say they were *at last* free when they had never been tied?

> I was speaking rhetorically. In fact I care for you very
> much but in a way that is of no interest to you. I now

think of you as an expensive car I cannot afford—and
even were it given to me I would trade it in for a
different model.

He placed his pen at the interesting angle again and tried to
imagine Michelle reading the letter. Her jaw dropping in
shock. Her eyes welling with tears. Her wounded cry as she
rushed to the doll's room, fell to her knees and, sobbing,
began stuffing pieces of the letter into the chewed mouths
of her dolls. Meanwhile her telephone would be ringing,
perhaps it would be Sol looking for a return engagement.
But no, how could she speak to anyone while her heart
twisted in grief and torment—

All right. Maybe grief and torment was going too far.
Perhaps her heart would simply be muffled in a blanket of
grey sadness. And instead of a wounded cry there might be
only a short bitter laugh, the French-movie laugh that the
camera always followed briefly before switching to someone else, usually smoking a cigarette and looking indiffer-
ently into the distance.

Aaron tore up his letter to Michelle, then took a magazine across the street where it kept him company while he
had a steak and frites with a small pitcher of red wine. After
dinner he began to walk. How bad could life be when your
main job was eating, drinking and writing letters you would
never send to women you would never understand? He
turned his mind to the strange project he had been hatching
ever since the Jean-Louis phone call, a short autobiographi-
cal film about his visit to Paris. Such a film would need
action, so he decided to do something: he went into a bar
and stood at the counter to order a cognac. It was one of
those moments when strangers begin talking to each other.

Soon he was chatting with a young couple who had stopped for a drink on the way home from a disastrous visit to the woman's mother.

When he left the bar it was midnight. Drinks had been exchanged, hands had been shaken, cheeks had been kissed. As he zigzagged towards his place he suddenly found himself standing outside Michelle's apartment. Her lights were on, which was unexpected because she was supposed to be in Marseille, and then he saw her silhouetted against the lace sheers. She turned in profile. Her mouth was moving and he could hear the sound of her screaming though at first he couldn't make out the words. Another figure appeared, a man's, and he seemed almost threatening as he approached Michelle.

"Get out," Michelle cried.

The man retreated. Aaron stepped deeper into the shadows. Michelle was still at the window. A few seconds later the courtyard door to Michelle's building opened and the man Aaron had seen in the window emerged. He was wide-shouldered and walked with a slight limp, but quickly crossed the street and went round the corner without looking back. Michelle stayed at the window. When he had disappeared, she raised her hands to her face, as though sobbing, turned her back and left the room.

The next morning Aaron called her twice, both times leaving messages when her machine came on. He was out buying a present for Rose when he saw a florist. *Send her flowers*. He signed both his name and Rose's to the card.

A few hours later he was in Michelle's area again. From the point of view of the film he was planning—it had evolved in his mind into one of those charming little *auteur*-driven masterpieces on the seam between fact and fiction that substitute a wistful lightness of touch for the heavy drums of melodrama—it would be good to have a shot of him standing in the same place, looking in all the innocence of daylight at the window that last night revealed Michelle's terrible storm.

At the same time, Aaron felt there was something insidious, perhaps even immoral, about the way he was intruding on her privacy. Yes, he had bought her flowers, but he was spying on Michelle, he had to admit to himself, spying on her through a lens tinted with malice and jealousy. Not, he realized, because of Sol or the wide-shouldered man with the sinister limp; no, the real source of his jealousy was that he envied her ability to go still inside—to play dead. That gap in himself, that inner emptiness, was something he kept trying to fill with the boy he should have been. Michelle was stronger and more ambitious. Into her emptiness she would suck the energies of the universe, until the cords of power lay before her, waiting to be pulled. He himself, Aaron realized, would never have the strength to control others by either inner or outer silence. That was why it drove him —and probably everyone else she knew—crazy when she didn't answer the phone or return calls. That was why he had sent her flowers: not to cheer her up or placate her, but in tribute.

As he reached the corner he saw the flashing blue light of the police car and then the yellow ambulance light. He arrived at the entranceway only a moment before the stretcher emerged from the courtyard. There was a sheet over the body and two blue canvas straps held it in place, but as they were lifting the stretcher into the back of the ambulance the sheet caught and was tugged back. One day Aaron would telephone Sol to tell him about Michelle.

Through a connection at the prefecture, Sol would discover the exact chemical composition of the sleeping pills Michelle had used to kill herself. But at the moment he saw her body on the stretcher, the question of murder or suicide didn't enter Aaron's mind: he saw only the dolls, bitten and abused, and Michelle's face as it emerged from beneath the sheet, the parallel scarlet scratch marks gouged so deep they were almost troughs, where in some final desperate gesture Michelle had drawn her nails from her cheekbones down to her chin. He skin was pallid, her mouth pinched in mock severity. It was, this death mask, exactly the look Aaron had seen on her face while she listened to the answering machine—the perfect solemn stillness that would only break when she exploded into laughter.

When it came time to make the movie, Aaron cut the fact he had bought her flowers, because the arrival of the florist van just as the ambulance drove away was the kind of sentimental detail he had decided was no longer possible.

inventing
dostoyevsky

1

ONE DAY I FIND the word Dostoyevsky parked in my mind like a train in an empty station. A dusty steam train with a large black engine that is already sending up puffs of smoke, an overloaded coal car behind it, then a string of passenger cars of a dark smudged maroon with old-fashioned windows, some propped open, others tightly closed as though painted in place forever.

Each of the passenger cars is labelled with a letter of Dostoyevsky's name. I walk into the "O." Or perhaps it is the "Y." Dostoyevsky sits alone. He is wearing a ruined frock coat, a wrinkled black garment drawn tightly around his narrow shoulders, and stained baggy trousers that stink of piss, mud and spilled cheap wine that is turning to vinegar under the worst possible circumstances. His head is bent over a book and the skin beneath his eyes makes dark patches that come down to meet the top of his untrimmed beard. As he leans forward to cough he slams his right fist into his chest, as though to distract himself from his pain. I take the seat opposite him. When he looks up at me, I see that his pupils occupy an unnatural proportion of his eyes.

His gaze is equally unnatural; too strong, hypnotic, filled with a black sparkle that unlike every-thing else about him radiates a cheerfully arrogant self-confidence.

"I know you," those eyes are saying, "but you don't dare know me."

"You fool!" I wish my eyes would reply, "exactly the opposite is the case." Instead my eyes turn away from Dostoyevsky because, to tell the truth, knowledge cannot contain what is between us.

The train is moving now, perhaps it began long ago, through flat, patchily harvested fields of grain, small cottages, low thatch-roofed log barns. When it comes to a sudden stop Dostoyevsky is thrown into my arms, a sour steely bundle with sharp elbows and a harsh bristly beard. He pushes himself away and begins brushing obsessively at his trousers, as though he had an appointment with the Czar.

Dostoyevsky and I. In this car, the "O" or possibly the "Y," we are the only passengers. I am looking out the window and he is pretending to read his book.

The train has started again. From the empty station in a small blurred town we have passed onto a vast rolling prairie. The train is moving slowly and now I see that rising up from the horizon and running towards us is a huge army of brightly dressed peasants, waving for us to stop. "They are happiness," Dostoyevsky says. "If they are real, you and I have no reason to exist."

2

I can tell you the exact moment my innocence was lost. It was when, lifting up the cover of her dressing table in search of some cosmetic clue to her recent erratic behaviour, I discovered a picture of Fyodor Dostoyevsky taped to the corner of my mother's mirror.

The fierce patriarchal face dominated by its long black beard, its prominent aquiline nose, its black eyes bulging with nationalism and fanatic hatreds glared out at me as if to scream one word: *Impostor!*

How could I—a sickly envious child once described as "the feeble spawn of a deluded city's most laughable literary ringmaster"—even pretend to know anything of this great epileptic genius whose animus had roared out of the past and into the present where it had buried itself securely in that very place between my mother's legs from which I had so reluctantly emerged?

How much easier to deal with the dead than grapple with the living. The flaws and contradictions that so inconvenience life sparkle like jewels by the time the corpse is stiff. A few scandalous affairs? They make for good letters and provide the biographer's lash with some badly needed exercise. A drunken brawl or two? Reasons to speculate that such and such a writer, guilty of excesses we need not mention here, suffered at least one poetic moment, the poetic justice of pain and humiliation, the sudden gasping exhalation caused by a sharp boot being driven into the gut, the vulnerable helplessness of a slow-motion collapse when muscles are incapable of moving and the jaw simply hangs open like a landed fish submissively awaiting the next blow —or, better, like a freshly printed book after its first catastrophic review. A few weeks or decades of miserable poverty? A tendency to lionize, exaggerate, minimize, fantasize, enter periods of undeniable insanity or prolonged neurosis? Greatness is not processed cheese. A few disappointed or possibly even suicidal wives, husbands, lovers? Children traumatized or ignored or exiled or terrified? All grist for the academic mill. Everyone knows that generals and artists are not household pets.

And yet the appearance of the man himself, the skinny, raving, raggedly clothed lunatic full of foul humours and insults—how repulsive!—although it turns out he has a certain sleazy understanding that borders on a kind of twilight charm. He turns out to be someone with whom you are at first horrified to be sharing a minute, a drink, a table, a bed—then find yourself so flattered, so admired, so listened to, so *understood* and even *exalted*, that in the end you realize the bad reputation was all a misunderstanding. After a few bottles of wine followed by a cognac or three, the legend, even the living legend, turns out to be quite a good fellow, a worthy companion, an admittedly shiftless sort who nevertheless combines an excellent education with an astounding capacity for drink and a willingness to completely destroy himself for the pleasure of your company. I remember that night, you'll later tell your friends, though unlike the living legend you're not desperate to repeat it because you also remember the morning after.

Of course there are exceptions. Dostoyevsky's wife, Mary Magdalene, Leonard Woolf, my mother.

The way some do sidewalk sketches or quick clay busts, I could offer heart figures. Your heart is like a bag of popcorn, I could say, those who touch it always end up licking salt off their fingers and needing a drink.

I was supposed to be a historian by trade: trolling a narrative line through the random debris of the past was my designated future. I still live in the old section of the city, down by the lake where the streets were once a muddy cart-filled criss-cross linking taverns, offices and warehouses to the homes of the rich who owned them and the poor who made them function. The mud has been replaced by pavement, and the log building that originally occupied this site rebuilt into a six-storey warehouse since converted into offices and studios.

Sitting at my work table I have the view that is the reason I am here: framed by my window, as perfect as any picture but constantly changing. Central to the scene is a certain eighteenth-century greystone building. Low and wide, with an old-fashioned slate roof and small lead-paned windows that face north, it is currently a home for the homeless, a run-down squat for whoever can break in.

But when I was a child this building was an important landmark. At that time it was regarded as a heritage building and was known as the City Institute for the Literarily Insane.

The year I entered high school, in a ritual familiar to every schoolchild in our city, my class was bused to the institute for what the authorities must have decided was a useful cautionary inoculation against what my father used to call "the writing disease."

That day a dozen or more buses were lined up on the street outside the institute. The inmates—at that time the current system of using random government grants to alternately destabilize and dehospitalize artists had not yet been initiated—must have known we were coming. Banners had been hung outside the sooty windows: Words Not Turds, My Poem Is my Home, Say It with Flowers and other such nonsense greeted the unprepared eye. One entire floor was chanting, in ragged unison, what I later learned was an obscene Allen Ginsberg poem. From other opened windows frustrated authors poured forth their endless reams of disjointed text, their unappreciated stories, their poems of heartbreak, sunset, panic of the soul.

There must have been hundreds of us assembled that morning on the sidewalk. An almost equal number of inmates had their heads out the windows and, aside from those chanting, reading, shouting, etc., there were dozens who contented themselves with throwing out pamphlets, manuscripts, word-covered paper airplanes, remainders. Whoever said the pen was mightier than the sword must have been envisioning the kind of terrifying assault to which we were subjected.

Just as the voices began to grow hoarse, the Director appeared in the doorway. Of medium height and quite stocky, with one shoulder swollen and deformed by a lifetime of writing letters by hand, he had a look that seemed to me authoritative at the time, though afterwards I realized it was in fact apologetic.

There was a scattering of applause that made my heart race. The Director happened to be my father.

"Words would be superfluous," my father began.

"Your words would!" shouted a heckler.

My father instantly turned towards the offender and his long arm flashed out as he pointed at a disreputable bearded scarecrow. "Let him be seen," my father commanded.

We schoolchildren shifted uneasily. Was this some kind of staged event intended to warn us against the dangers of insubordination? The uncertainty grew as the inmate, wearing the alphabet-soup-style pyjamas that were the institute's uniform, was dragged onto a balcony by two burly guards.

"Name?" my father demanded.

"Fyodor Dostoyevsky!" cried the scarecrow. Then he cackled and there was loud applause from the windows. Skinny, black-bearded and in pyjamas, he seemed insubstantial between the scowling guards.

"Tell these brutes to let go of me. I cannot speak unless I am free."

My father nodded and the guards stepped back. "Now tell us your real name."

"Fyodor Mikhailovich Dostoyevsky. Are you deaf?" screamed the scarecrow and this time the windows erupted in laughter and applause.

My father turned to us schoolchildren, called upon to witness this impromptu morality play.

"Look at this man," my father instructed us. "He could have had a wife and family. A home with wall-to-wall carpets. A car with a cigarette lighter. But no, that wasn't enough, was it?"

"It would be *nothing*," moaned Dostoyevsky.

"*Nada, Nada, Nada!*" the other inmates chanted. Surely this show was planned. All the children laughed and instead of being ashamed of my father I began to be proud of the way he handled himself as an actor.

"It would have been life," my father corrected in his fine stentorian voice. "Without carpets, you have the bare floor. Without the floor, you have dirt. Without dirt, you have oblivion." I realized my father had given himself the best part.

"Why am I here?" Dostoyevsky screamed.

"Why is he here?" the other inmates chorused.

"You know perfectly..." my father began.

But now no one was listening to my father. Our eyes were on Dostoyevsky, who had pulled off his alphabet-soup shirt and thrown it to the street. His chest was pale and consumptive, his long arms corded with effort as he grasped the rail of the balcony.

"Don't worry," my father reassured us, "he is harmless."

Dostoyevsky climbed over the railing and stood on the ledge. All he now wore was his pyjama bottom. For some reason my eyes were fixed on his large feet, the way his toes curled for balance on the stone sill. All his message was in those toes, their constant strained flexing. Later in life I was told great actors can use any part of their body to communicate their feelings and I instantly thought of the anxious desperate cramping of those toes on that fall afternoon that would have been perfect for a carefree picnic or a sleep on sun-warmed grass.

"Harmless," Dostoyevsky repeated in a voice filled with sarcasm and bitterness. His toes had stopped and he was pointing down accusingly at my father. Even so long ago, my father was not a young man. He had iron-grey hair, tortoiseshell glasses, a long unhappy face with cheeks carved up by life's disappointments. Along with his permanently humped shoulder and the odd way it forced him to hold his head there was also something strange in his gait, a kind of stiff-leggedness that, when he stood, made it appear he was about to topple over. "Look at him," Dostoyevsky commanded, "look at the idiot," and when he spoke his long accusing arm grew longer yet. "Of all the stupid things he has said, and believe me, my young friends, his ignorant pronouncements could fill an encyclopedia, calling me or any other inmate here *harmless* is the most stupid of all."

Such was the scornful certainty that filled Dostoyevsky's voice, that we all—several hundred thirteen-year-olds including one, me, who was the son of the idiot in question, nodded in agreement.

"Harmless. I'll show you harmless." Then, stripping off his alphabet-soup pyjama bottoms, Dostoyevsky crushed the material until it had entirely disappeared between his large knotted hands. Now entirely naked, he held his joined fists towards us, like a magician seeking our attention for his next trick. Suddenly he spread his hands apart and, snapping forth and waving the alphabet pyjama like the carefree flag of a country only he could belong to, Dostoyevsky jumped.

3

(From a speech given in 1952 by Albert Pace, Director of the City Institute for the Literarily Insane)

The sad fact is that despite the apparent glamour of his or her designation, the literary executor faces a lippery black cliff that can only induce despair. In some badly kept room or bulging trunk he comes across the writer's unpublished and unpublishable remains. The vast mount of paper left behind by a writer in mid- or late career should not be underestimated. Nor its disorder. But while burdened by the duty of sorting through the thick clods of discarded drafts, randomly saved letters and clippings, beginnings without endings and endings without beginnings, etc., the executor has also to keep in mind an even more difficult task: the dead writer, who while alive burned with inescapable ambitions even more irrational than the most disordered box of papers, has made the executor responsible for the impossible Stygian task of transporting the departed writer's oeuvre from past to posterity.

Literature's most famous executor is Max Brod. When Franz Kafka died of tuberculosis in Berlin in 1924, he was impoverished and virtually unknown in either Germany or his native Czechoslovakia. He left behind him *The Trial* and *The Castle*—two of the century's great masterpieces—unpublished. His instructions to Max Brod, his longtime friend and admirer, were to destroy them.

Instead Brod decided to publish them and in Kafka's case the trip across the literary Styx was entirely a success. Even today, more than seventy years after Kafka's death, not only are his books known worldwide, but the initial "K" has become an icon of enormous symbolic significance. Kafka, as a critic cruelly said—and being myself a critic I revel in the cruel sayings of my colleagues—has graduated from being an author to a brand name.

After Kafka's example, what writer—ignored and possibly even belittled in his or her own time—could be satisfied with the prospect of her work following her into the grave? Posthumous fame has become, in their minds at least, the just destiny of every scribbler. No wonder they search with such care for a literary executor who can accomplish after their deaths what they themselves have failed to achieve during their lifetimes.

In my own case, I suppose that my official position made me a natural target for such wounded aspirations. I cannot, in this brief talk, detail all the circumstances under which I have encountered the sordid remnants of lives "devoted to the pen" (to quote a favourite patient) but even though I managed to bring a few works into the public eye through private publication at my own expense, the very eccentricities that had driven the poor authors into my care invariably tainted the works themselves, limiting them to being at best—the worst cannot even be discussed—nothing more than well-wrought symptoms of minds gone awry.

You may protest that many of the world's literary greats have been unstable. Yes, I agree, even very unstable, but during their productive periods, their instability was a bicycle they were capable of riding. Otherwise, unfortunately, I am afraid that my decades of experience have led me to believe that meritorious artistic production is a direct function of mental health.

In order to give scientific weight to this unique proposition, I devised a series of tests which I would now like to describe in some detail . . .

4

After a week of treatment in City Hospital, Dostoyevsky was released with only a few bruises and a walking cast on his left foot as souvenirs of his unusual escape. To my embarrassment, the episode had made the newspapers, and my mother insisted Dostoyevsky be brought into our home to finish his recuperation.

"You drove him to it," she said to my father, "now we have to help him."

Dostoyevsky was installed in the guest room, a chamber originally designated for the siblings I was intended to have. Early in the morning, before I left for school, Dostoyevsky would sometimes limp into the hall. His cast, half hidden by the grey sweatpants my mother had bought him, clomped noisily on the hardwood floor and as he came into the light—the angle of his door must have caused the shadows to behave strangely—his face would appear to be glistening with tears.

One morning that Dostoyevsky stayed in his room, my father went to work early and I was left alone in the kitchen with my mother. She was reading the paper, paying no attention to me at all except to say, as I finished my cereal, "Jonathan, this one time, please rinse your bowl."

"We should get a dishwasher," I said sulkily.

"Your father says it's a waste of money and energy." She got up and took out the electric mixer, which I knew meant she would now start making waffles for Dostoyevsky.

"If it's such a waste to have a dishwasher, isn't it a waste to make waffles when half the world is starving?"

"Would you like to be dead?" my mother proposed.

"No thanks."

"Then figure it out for yourself."

By this time I had learned some of the "facts" of Dostoyevsky's case. Apparently an actual descendant of the Russian writer and legally entitled to his name, the man in question claimed to have been given, by God, the task of actually rewriting the original's works.

Sitting at his table in the guest room—did I mention that for years it had been furnished with a crib and bassinet?—Dostoyevsky would spend hours every day laboriously copying his ancestor's oeuvre. My mother bought him a set of quill pens along with a supply of pure India ink. The high-pitched scratching of steel nibs could be heard through the whole house.

"What's so wonderful about copying?" I asked my mother one day. "Why doesn't he make something up for himself?"

"That," my mother pronounced, her voice thick with pleasure, "is the right question. Do you know that in the Middle Ages there were hundreds of monasteries filled with monks who spent every day growing closer to God by copying out the Bible?"

"I saw it in a movie. Is Dostoyevsky a monk?"

"His own kind of monk," my mother said. "But I believe his suffering is authentic."

It turned out that Dostoyevsky had some sort of disease, or perhaps it was part of his trauma, that caused him to be ravenous at all times. If my mother was out, she would have left him a plate of something in the refrigerator: either Russian specialities like cabbage rolls and kasha with noodles, or delicacies they had discovered in their trips to the supermarket—Rice Krispie squares, vegetable oil crackers, processed cream cheese with red and green pimentos.

If she was in the house his scratching would be accompanied by the sounds and smells of her cooking. She would come up to his room carrying a tray with chicken soup and black bread. Then she would call out cheerily: "Prisoner Dostoyevsky, your rations have arrived. Please allow the guard into your cell."

Sometimes when she closed the door behind her she would seem to be annoyed. "Prisoner Dostoyevsky, I believe you are again contravening weapon regulations."

At first I presumed this meant that instead of copying, the sound of scratching was Dostoyevsky filing his quills into miniature knives. Trying to fall asleep, I was afraid that during the night Dostoyevsky would attack our innocent sheltering family with his homemade weapons.

Later I learned my mother's admonition was the prelude —when I wasn't home—to strip searches and intense physical explorations during which Dostoyevsky would conceal his favourite weapon in my mother. I would arrive back from school and find them in the kitchen sucking tea through sugar cubes, eating pickled herring along with crackers and cream cheese and talking with unnatural vivacity about the glories of riding across the snow-covered steppes. When I read my mother's diary I found out that too had its corresponding reality: one of their prison games was playing horsie, an activity for which my mother provided an illustration, although such was her modesty that even in this personal diary her breasts were covered by Dostoyevsky's hands.

A certain anxiety invaded our household. Nights when my father was not at meetings or tending to various of his official duties, he and Dostoyevsky would sit after dinner in the living room and have tense discussions about politics and literature.

As Dostoyevsky's health improved, and his relations with my mother deepened, he grew ever more aggressive with my father. One night he leapt to his feet, livid with fury, and for the first time actually raised his voice in our house. Suddenly we were back to the afternoon I first saw him at the asylum, the whole world reduced to a black chasm separating this raving monster with the power of the universe in his frenzy from the immovable will of my cold and deformed father.

"*Listen!*" Dostoyevsky shouted. "Listen and learn." He pulled a crumpled sheet of paper from his trousers and read: "'The direct, legitimate fruit of consciousness is iner-tia. Men of action are active only because they are stupid and limited.'"

My father stood immobile, his mouth open, his entire body apparently turned to stone or in the midst of a heart attack. Then he slumped back into his chair. "You sound so sure of yourself," he mumbled. "How can you be so certain about such things?"

"Of course I am certain," Dostoyevsky trumpeted. "I'm quoting myself." He waved the paper triumphantly. "*Notes from Underground*, page 139. Haven't you even read my books? I thought I was your enemy."

"I read them," my father said. "Most of them. But I didn't memorize them. Or maybe it was a different translation. Now I remember something like: 'Thought is sleep. Only those who remain awake can change the world.'"

"Slogans," Dostoyevsky spat contemptuously. "When they reduce your greatness to slogans, expect the mediocre at your door."

"When I opened my door," my father said, "you were the one I saw."

"I have nothing to prove to you," Dostoyevsky said haughtily. "But let me remind you of one detail. When some of my shorter novels were collected and published in America, the great Thomas Mann wrote the introduction. The Nobel Prize winner, the world's conscience."

"Spread it thick, comrade," my father said, in an ironic voice coloured by complex self-contradictions only he could fully appreciate.

"Of course you are jealous. Why shouldn't you be? But just imagine the great Thomas Mann, hiding from the war in California, sitting in the army boots and safari shorts that had been sent to him by his admirer Ernest Hemingway, trying to make a few pennies by turning his Olympian gaze on a poor wretch such as myself. If Thomas Mann, as pompous an ass as yourself, was capable of seeing my genius, perhaps you could learn to do the same."

"Spare me your boasting."

"Spare the boast and spoil the host. You know what Thomas Mann said about me? Of course the narcissist was speaking with reference to himself: 'The profound criminal-saintly face of Dostoyevsky appears only fleetingly in my writings.' If Thomas Mann called me saintly, who are you to complain?"

My father had slumped to one side in his chair and was leaning on his right elbow, his deformed shoulder presenting a lump almost equal in size to his head. Through the tears that had clouded my eyes he looked like Siamese twins.

"Admit you are jealous," Dostoyevsky insisted.

"I am jealous," said my father. "I know what you are doing with my wife. Today I resigned my post at the institute. Tomorrow I leave this house."

My mother's face went white and she sucked in her breath. Otherwise she remained silent and transfixed, utterly unmoved to act, as if this scene was part of an interesting movie that she happened to be watching.

"So! You leave in order to punish your wife for sleeping with me! What gives you the right to deny her the opportunity to be intimate with a world-historic figure? A saint! And there is me to consider, my work. The great Dostoyevsky masterpieces cannot remain buried in the past and I am the one destined to bring them into the present and give them eternity. How do you expect genius to function without a muse? What a cynic you are. No wonder they call you the literary executioner!"

My father knotted his hands together and loudly cracked his knuckles. Finally my mother flinched, jerking at the sound of my father's joints as though she were being lashed.

I went upstairs and closed my bedroom door. I finished my homework and packed my knapsack for school. There was a bottle of aspirins on my desk. I took them all. When I woke up it was noon. My pillow was soaked in vomit and the house was empty.

5

What is missing so often is the woman's voice. Touch, some say. So call me the evil mistress. Got him in my house then gave him what he craved, that famous woman's touch, and after touching came the voice. Mine. *Your thing is like a stick of dynamite*, I wrote. I would have said anything—it was only to make him happy. "I suppose I am meant to be flattered," he said, "but it makes me afraid to go off." My first instinct was flash. Now I stick to images I find in the kitchen.

My son. *Oy!* Isn't that what mothers are supposed to say? First my son was horrified when I sought out sex, then he felt the same way about money. Who wouldn't want money? Money money money. So I have a silk scarf around my neck. Would I be a better person if I wore a paper towel?

Once I did try to be a better person. Years after Albert moved to the apartment, I temporarily forgot everything, and I came to visit Albert so I could crawl back into his favour. This was for the boy's sake. Albert was sitting in judgment behind his desk, as though waiting for me to speak so he could write it down in his famous memoirs.

I got down on my hands and knees and set out to cross the carpet, pass underneath his desk and undo his pants.

Did I really care what he had inside? Did I really want to give it my famous woman's touch? Or even use it as a microphone so it could hear my famous woman's voice?

All I wanted was to abase myself. I wanted to make myself so dirty he would need to forgive me.

But his carpet! It was filthy! I would have wrapped him in my hair, slung him in my tongue.... But his carpet! His carpet! With each lurch forward—people love to boast about crawling yet there is no word for the distance travelled in one forward movement of the knee while the rest of the body trails behind like an overgrown baby blanket—clouds of dust rose into my face. Before I could manage his zipper I succumbed to a fit of coughing. I staggered to my feet, stumbled to a chair where I continued to cough until finally Albert brought me a glass of water. By the time I had wiped my face, taken control of my breathing, the moment for romance, even vulgar romance, had passed.

Meanwhile, Albert was now on *his* knees. You would think I would be happy to see my husband, the so-called victim, kneeling in front of the one he had so falsely accused. Justice at last. But I have never liked looking down on Albert. Over the years his black hair has turned grey and receded to a carefully brushed V and this development has only emphasized what I always found so uncomfortable about Albert's head from above, the inescapable vista of his enormous skull.

What is inside Albert's huge head?

Among other things, towering over the rest of the trivia like a large piece of furniture locked in a closet, a cross-referenced catalogue of every one of my misdeeds.

"For the boy's sake," Albert said, "get the criminal out of your life."

The boy, the boy. I had him, I loved him, I did my best. But what about me? The voice cries out but there is no echo. Except, in the beginning, with D. When I cried out for mercy he would grunt and groan in return. The body has had its day. Wrung out, exorcised, brought to a fever pitch. Whatever words must be assigned to the writhing hellion I became, the evil mistress found her glory. At the end of a man's stick, you will say, traitor to your sex, you should have crossed your legs and meditated.

From *oy* to *om*. In the end the dynamite didn't go off, it just went away. I left him for someone rich, which is almost the same thing. When we do it now it isn't. The same. We're too alike. Greedy ferrets crawling up the trousers of life in the hope of a few choice morsels. Siblings in sin, we've actually become fond of each other. Sometimes we just lie on his bed—not even undressing though I always take off my jewellery—talking about this and that until one of us falls asleep.

6

When Dostoyevsky called my father "the literary executioner," there was a growl in the back of his throat I could feel resonating through my own body. The literary executioner—yes, I was the son of *that* man.

The night everything came out between Dostoyevsky and my parents was the twentieth of March. I remember because the homework I'd been assigned by my English teacher was to write a poem on the joys of spring.

I should explain here that after my father gave his speech on Max Brod, he used a small letterpress in our basement to print it up as a pamphlet. The pamphlet was so short it could be bound with a couple of stitches—my father performed this operation by hand. There was also a brown cardboard cover illustrated by a charcoal sketch drawn by my mother. In this image his long face was angular, almost cruel. I wondered if my father resented being portrayed this way, or if he simply thought that my mother wasn't much of an artist.

The Literary Executor was the title of my father's pamphlet and I was sent to distribute it to a list of bookstores which had agreed to take it on consignment.

Normally such an amateur production would not have attracted public notice. However, given the dubious status conferred by my father's official position, every major newspaper carried a prominent and unflattering review of *The Literary Executor*.

The main result was that behind his back my father became known as "the literary executioner." Dostoyevsky had pronounced these words with a predatory snarl that made me tingle. Others drew less reaction, except for my English teacher who would discharge such witticisms as "Now, would the executioner's son be so kind as to enlighten us on Shakespeare's intentions in the second scene of the third act," etc., and with my face burning I would be forced to stammer out some reply.

Under these circumstances, the prospect of writing a poem that would be introduced to the class as "an example of guillotine rhyme" or "the hangman's sonnet" or some equally laboured witticism was less than appealing.

On a piece of paper I wrote:

INVENTING DOSTOYEVSKY

Two parts shit
Three of bile
Helps our genius
Strut and smile

Every season
Smells the same
When Dostoyevsky
Is your name

Summer fall winter spring
Find a woman do your thing
Spring summer fall winter
Genius is the manic splinter
Drive it deep beneath the nail
Save your vomit for the pail

"This is an interesting step backwards," my teacher commented when I read the poem aloud in class. But there was a new wary note in his voice, as though something from Dostoyevsky had rubbed off on me and the teacher felt that if provoked I might turn the pail upside down on his head.

When I got home from school my mother was waiting in the living room. Suitcases had been packed and that very evening we flew to England. For several years we floated about the continent, at first living in what my mother liked to call "the penury of exile," then in a series of apartments and homes related in dubious ways to the gentlemen my mother had the knack of attracting.

By the time we returned I was a self-declared sophisticated youth halfway through university. I'd picked up smatterings of various languages, some Italian clothes, and visited a lot of cities that under other circumstances would have been delightful places to spend a few weeks or months. Aside from my so-called formal education, inflicted by constantly changing schools and the succession of tutors my mother hired in the hope I'd somehow make sense of the jigsaw puzzle she'd given me, I developed a love of old buildings. Buildings were easy. Buildings were beautiful. Buildings grew up in one place and stayed there.

The day after our arrival home I went to see my father. He had sold the house and moved downtown to one of those shabby declining mansions that are bought up and subdivided by real estate speculators. His apartment was above the quadruple garage that served the other tenants.

There is a photograph of me from that time: I look like a would-be private school boy—grey flannels, tailored blazer, pale blue shirt and tie. Knocking at my father's door I was conscious of the transcontinental fellow I had become, and wondered how he would react to me. Following my knock there was a long silence during which I worried that I had mistaken the time. Then came his agonizingly slow step, a fumbling at the latch.

The door swung open. My father had backed away to avoid having to embrace me. I didn't rush after him. While I'd been gathering my bits of wardrobe and foreign phrases, my father—the stern authoritarian figure whose every movement once embodied his iron will had become a shambling frail creature I instantly felt compelled to take care of.

His apartment was a single large room with the kitchen and bathroom sectioned off by walls that stopped short of the ceiling. A hundred years ago it had probably been a gaming and billiards room. More recently, judging from the splashes on the floor, it had served as an artist's studio.

"Good to see you," I said awkwardly.

My father's face twitched and tears started at the corners of his eyes. But he didn't speak.

"I hope you always keep your windows open," I said ridiculously. "Living up here, above the garage, you could get poisoned by the exhaust. I read about a case like that in the newspaper."

"Never mind," he said. "I'm writing a memoir that has become my whole life."

All along one wall my father had built a set of bookshelves. He was not much of a carpenter and, crammed with the materials he needed, they looked as though they'd suffered from a serious earthquake. In front of them were the sawhorses he'd used, bridged by a few unpainted boards themselves piled with books.

"Would you mind if I tried reading you a few passages?" he asked.

He had taken nothing from the house for the apartment. His furnishings consisted of the wall of bookshelves, his sawhorses, something that might have been an army cot, the dilapidated armchair in which I was sitting, and a magnificent oak dining table behind which he now placed himself. His deformed shoulder was swollen even further by the task of filling the stacks of pages he had arranged in front of himself like the crenellated tower of his own personal literary castle.

"I'd be honoured," I said.

My father stood up again, a sheaf of papers rattling in his hand. The sound cut through me and I suddenly turned towards the window, certain I would see Dostoyevsky. There was nothing but the branches of a weed maple and a tangle of wires.

"'I have given my life to literature,'" my father began.

Now is when you kill him, I heard Dostoyevsky say. I couldn't tell if he was speaking from inside me or if his voice, an insistent whisper, was coming from some corner of the room. *Don't let him start. Leap to your feet. Knock him over. Choke him. You're strong enough now.*

"'But the years of my childhood are all the happiness I have ever known,'" my father said.

What about you? Dostoyevsky whispered. *Does he hate you so much he doesn't count his only child among his blessings? Put your hands around your neck. You won't be free until you learn to murder him.*

"'In those days, it seemed, the sun shone brighter, and winter snow stayed clean until the spring.'"

Mercy, groaned Dostoyevsky. Now I was able to see his cynical shadow against the glass. He must have been on the roof the whole time.

"'And spring indeed was my favourite season, when my mother would come in from the garden smelling of earth and flowers.'"

Oh, God have mercy. Smelling of earth and flowers. Sounds like a corpse. At least he could have her smelling of whisky and sex.

Visits to my father were regular, if infrequent, but it was a long time before I saw Dostoyevsky, at least in the flesh. Nonetheless, I was constantly reminded of him. Every few weeks I opened the newspaper and his name—sometimes even his picture—would be there, over a review of some foreign novel or the biography of a nineteenth-century author his ancestor would have known. Once he even reviewed a biography about the real Dostoyevsky—a multi-volumed work which, he complained, made no reference to himself. Soon after, he was featured on a small segment of a television show which included an interview with a Russian specialist who afterwards declared that this reincarnated Dostoyevsky, whoever he was, had an unmatched knowledge of nineteenth-century Russia and Russian literature. He was then given his own weekly column, and his harsh guttural voice became common on the radio.

I will admit it—my life was poisoned by Dostoyevsky. I would go the reference library and hunt down every one of his clippings. When he received an inconsequential part-time appointment to the university's Russian department, I went to spy and even glanced into his office early one morning at an hour when I knew he would still be asleep.

Finally I could no longer resist. My need to re-encounter Dostoyevsky had become an unstoppable obsession. It was as though I truly believed Dostoyevsky possessed the very essence I required. From my mother I got the address of his apartment, but on the day I decided to visit it, I spotted him in a café. His face had taken on weight, and his beard puffed out from it like a white cloud. He was wearing a trench coat that spread out over his shoulders and arms like a tent as he hunched over a newspaper, smoking a cigarette and staring at the print with his head down and his wire-rimmed glasses shoved halfway down his nose.

Before I could decide what to do, Dostoyevsky's eyes swung up from his newspaper and focused on me. There was a moment of incomprehension, and I thought he was going to look away, but suddenly he was waving me towards him, his hand working and his chin arcing up and down as though he knew my fears and was trying to assure me that *yes*, I was wanted.

Once—after my mother had told my father that she intended to enter the world of free love, but before that fateful evening in the living room that finished off our family—she came home from one of her "encounters" with her face so red I thought she must have caught some disease. I was standing in the hall looking up anxiously at her as she took off her coat, and some intimation of the truth about her colouring must have struck home. It sliced through me, almost like its own kind of orgasm, and for that moment it was as if my mother and I were naked in every way. Then the knowledge receded and something else came to take its place, some sort of substitute like a particular bird's song or the smell of snow melting off pavement.

As I came up, Dostoyevsky put away his paper and set his hands on the table as though they were a deck of cards we were going to be playing with. It was over ten years since we had last met. The skin on Dostoyevsky's hands had started to turn papery and for the first time I saw him not only as a dark and irresistible rival to my father, but as a man who had been drawn into the kingdom of the elderly.

"*Jonathan*." Dostoyevsky said my name in such a familiar way I could almost believe he was glad to see me. Meanwhile the waitress had come to stand beside us and as I ordered my coffee she stared down at Dostoyevsky. She had a scattering of freckles across her face, was tall and long-legged with auburn hair whose softness I couldn't help imagining against my cheek. It came to me that the waitress might be experiencing a similar attraction to me. Perhaps my need to meet Dostoyevsky had been the disguise for a larger and more significant synchronicity, the grand event of my first real love affair. I wondered what the waitress would think when I told her the real truth about this man. We would be in bed, sheets up to our necks, exchanging this and other confidences after a session of cataclysmic love-making. But how would we get from here to there? The time had come for me to break the silence, but Dostoyevsky spoke first.

"How are you doing?" he asked her. "I didn't recognize you."

"How are *you*?" she asked, and then put a long-fingered hand on his shoulder.

After she left, Dostoyevsky explained that the waitress was a doctoral student who was doing her thesis on the subject of his early short stories.

I could tell her something, I wanted to say. But what? That she should have been mine? That Dostoyevsky's pretentiousness had ruined my parents' lives? "Someone's writing a book about my father," I finally replied. That person was, of course, my father himself.

"He deserves it," Dostoyevsky said quickly. "A man like your father is not to be underestimated, believe me, I have a lot of respect for him. His only problem was anarchism. He had no response to anarchism."

"And what about you?" I asked. The waitress was again standing above us, greedily sucking in our conversation. My initial attraction to her was already history. I thought she must be one of, I could only imagine, hundreds of Dostoyevsky acolytes scattered through the city.

What I meant by my question was that my father's problem had been not anarchism but Dostoyevsky and his manipulative behaviour. Like one of his own nihilistic and unscrupulous characters, Dostoyevsky had plotted his way into my mother's bed as though it was the most natural thing in the world that a raving lunatic should end up between the sheets of a prosperous married woman with familial responsibilities and a modicum of taste. "Excuse me," I said to the waitress, "but you are a student of literature. You must be familiar with Tolstoy's *Anna Karenina*. Do you remember the way she betrayed her husband for that pretentious soldier who thought he was an artist? And what art did he give her? The opportunity to end her life by throwing herself in front of a train. Great drama! Thank you! And think of the son! Had he not died of grief he could have known she had killed herself over a fool. A spiritual brother of the fraud for whom the height of achievement is to find himself ordering a coffee from a waitress who has performed a doctoral dissection of his early stories. Count me out."

"That's a fascinating point of view," the waitress said. "The voice from the margin. Tell me, how did you feel when your mother killed herself?"

"I was speaking in metaphors. It's the principle that counts."

"What I can't handle is the misery," Dostoyevsky said. "Suffering. It makes me blind to everything else. You are in a dark cave. You see a light. The light is goodness. You would do anything to escape the darkness, to be near that light, to be good even for a few moments. Nothing else matters. And then, of course, who am I to tell the light where to shine? The light has its own laws. Don't underestimate your mother, she knew what she was doing."

"My mother has changed," I said bitterly. "She used to

prostitute herself for art. Now she is only interested in money."

I couldn't believe these words had fallen from my mouth. I felt embarrassed and ashamed, as though the waitress had told me right to my face that she would prefer someone like Dostoyevsky, even if he had entered the kingdom of the elderly, to a shallow spiteful child like myself.

7

Shortly after I had started seeing Dostoyevsky again, my father telephoned to ask me to bring Dostoyevsky to the apartment. He told me Dostoyevsky's answers to certain questions were necessary to complete his memoirs, and that my presence would "facilitate matters."

Today, sitting at my work table and looking out at the rain-slick slate roof of the building he once ruled, I can still close my eyes and hear my father booming out commands to Dostoyevsky and the guards. But I could never get used to his voice over the telephone. There was something wrong with the idea of him allowing himself to speak into a small piece of plastic. I imagine the man, the man my father was, standing alone in a room and consenting to humiliate himself in this way. I would have preferred that he write me a letter or even arrive unannounced at my door. That is something I have also had to leave to my imagination: my father in the various places I have lived. How would he appear lounging this way or that, on what exact note would he occupy a certain kitchen in which I would be making him a meal, a sitting room casually scattered with the books I was eager for him to associate with me? But he was the King. It was always I who made the journey.

The night before I was to make that journey with Dostoyevsky, I had my dream about the train. The ancient cars lettered with Dostoyevsky's name. Dostoyevsky's sharp and sour body in my arms. When I woke up I was sweating. The smells of the train had filled the room and as I stepped out of bed I slipped on a blanket and fell hard to the floor. I ended up on my back, skull ringing, one hip aching. I had a crazy idea: *Dostoyevsky* is *real—one way or another he is always on his back, body bruised, his vista a grey cracked ceiling vibrating to the weight of invisible boots.* When I got up I made myself coffee, then wrote down the dream, knowing it was incomplete.

On my way to collect Dostoyevsky I bought a bag of chocolate marshmallow cookies. As a child I always loved the sound of the thin chocolate coating cracking between my teeth—once I advertised this to my father and we stood in the kitchen and devoured an entire package, swooning with every bite to that sweet inspirational cadenza I can still hear and taste. For once my father and I were on the same wavelength. "What an optimistic world Proust might have created," he sighed, "if only his madeleine had been chocolate-wrapped marshmallow with a layer of strawberry jam atop the crushed wafer base."

We arrived early in the afternoon. I had imagined my father's interview with Dostoyevsky would take place over tea. Dostoyevsky was not at all nervous—in fact he was glowing. The previous weekend had seen a full-page review by him in the city's most prestigious newspaper. His byline had included the phrase "renowned critic and commentator," and Dostoyevsky had brought a copy to show off.

I knocked at the door. My father called for us to enter and, as always since the first visit following my return, I let myself in. My father was in his usual position: seated behind his desk peering out from the piled manuscripts of his memoirs which now covered not only most of his oak dining table, but much of the floor. Today, however, there was a variation. In a chair drawn up beside the table, as elegant and beautifully kept as my father was awkward and dilapidated, sat my mother. But at Dostoyevsky's entrance my father was the one who shone with triumph, while my mother—despite the equally shiny shell of her lacquered hair and the burnt-ochre silk suit set off with an emerald brooch that her elegance and beauty had earned her in Paris—lowered her eyes.

There was a disagreeable moment as Dostoyevsky and I registered the situation. Dostoyevsky broke the silence. "Congratulations," he said to my father, "you've finally managed to surprise me."

My father's long face had grown predatory with the years, and a couple of recently lost teeth he hadn't bothered to replace left dark gaps in his smile.

"And I congratulate you," my father returned to Dostoyevsky. "After so many false starts you've finally made a success of yourself. Life as a fraud is treating you well."

"A fraud! So, you're still jealous. I thought we were past that but here we are, almost dead, and I'm still the worm twisting in your gut. Poor man. I should pity you. The literary executioner haunted by the guilt that eats him from the inside until he wakes up writhing. I can just see you twisted in your sheets, breathing hard and panting as though you'd finally managed to screw your own wife again."

My mother's cheeks burned and she started to rise. "Please. I never agreed to this."

"Don't tell me what you never agreed to," my father said. He turned to Dostoyevsky. "That bit about the wormy guilt wasn't bad. Did you get it from one of your books or did you actually make it up? Incidentally, I noticed you plagiarized your big review of the Tolstoy biography. I found it in a French magazine. One of these days you're going to be exposed."

"It was a question of saving time. Anyway, the French review read like a perfume advertisement."

"The perfume was the ending that you added on." My father pulled out his own copy of the clipping Dostoyevsky had shown me so proudly: "'History will judge Tolstoy's life as his only true creation. His novels, flawed and sentimental, will be forgotten and left in the shadows of his great contemporary.' Now I wonder who that might be? Surely not our honoured guest."

Dostoyevsky nodded, his face still smooth with the bliss of hearing his own words being read in my father's stentorian tones. "Yes, that exactly. Well put. You see, I didn't steal, I did what great writers do, which is to take what is written, improve it, then supply the necessary conclusion. You should be saying, 'Well done, Fodo, another brilliant excursion into the world of letters. Like Columbus, you discover continents, and the continents you discover are always unexpected.' You see, I have given you a rare privilege: a performance at which only you witnessed the backstage machinations."

I looked at my mother. Somehow we had allowed ourselves to be drawn into watching a rematch of the struggle that had taken place in our living room ten years before. Was this our welcome-home party? Or was my mother supposed to be calling her travel agent again?

"Gentlemen," my mother pleaded.

"Excuse me," my father apologized. He guided my mother back to her chair. From his jacket he took out a plastic vial and, in a gesture familiar since the earliest days of my childhood, shook some pills into the palm of his hand, the way he did when he had heart pains, and swallowed them without water. "Please, she is right. Let us let the past be past. I have brought you here together, the three people I have been closest to in my adult life, to celebrate the final chapter of my memoir."

"It's finished?" my mother asked.

We all looked about the room, as though we might discover a pile of freshly bound books.

"Done," said my father. "I wrote my last sentence a week ago."

"You've surprised me again," Dostoyevsky said. "I didn't think you had it in you."

"Don't worry," said my father, "it's in me. All of it." Then he asked my mother to make us a pot of tea so we might celebrate and, if not forgive each other, at least "allow the past to grow more distant."

These words from my father, framing the past as though a landscape receding through a window of a train, brought back in all its intensity the dream I'd had about Dostoyevsky. Once more I was in the train, unsure which car we occupied, Dostoyevsky and I. But now I knew this was a dream I had dreamed every night of my life.

"Look!" I exclaimed to Dostoyevsky. "This is just a dream—I even know what's going to happen. I've written it out." Dostoyevsky set down his book and watched as I pulled the pages from my pocket. I began to read: "'One day I find the word *Dostoyevsky* parked in my mind like . . .'"

"Wait," Dostoyevsky said. "You sound like a frightened boy. Read it again, with feeling."

"'One day I find the word *Dostoyevsky...*'"

"Stop! Listen to the way you read: "I find the word *Dostoyevsky...*' Are you dying of boredom as you recite the telephone book? Please. With feeling. 'I find THE WORD! *DOSTOYEVSKY!*' Say my name as though it means something!" He snatched the pages from me. "'Dostoyevsky sits alone...' Do you have any idea what that means? *Why* does Dostoyevsky sit alone? It is your dream. If he sits alone it is because you are afraid of him. And when you join him, why does Dostoyevsky agree to sit there with you? Since you obviously don't know, I will tell you. Dostoyevsky has his own plans. He is trading souls with you. If you are going to speak, speak with my voice. Listen. 'Dostoyevsky sits alone. He is wearing a ruined frock coat...'"

He turned the pages until he came to those I had left blank. "What happens here?"

"Those," I said, "are the parts of my dream I have never remembered. But now I do. We are on our way to a trial. The train is taking us to the courtroom where my father is the judge."

Dostoyevsky handed me back the pages. "You think someone pays me to be in your dreams, play juvenile games with your mother and fight with your blockhead of a father? Have you ever asked yourself what all this must be like for me?"

We were entering the outskirts of a small town. As the train slowed, gasping and exhaling steam, I had a tiny moment of feeling sorry for Dostoyevsky. But then, I realized, it wasn't as if *I* were writing his lines. Hadn't he just said that I would have to pay for his voice with my soul?

"You have your own life," I protested. "You live by your own rules."

"Please. Are you your father? Don't teach me philosophy until I sign up for the course."

When we got to the station Dostoyevsky and I left the car together. We were on a platform that fronted a small wooden station house. Its windows were cobwebbed, the door opened to an empty room that smelled of cheap tobacco. Both wickets were closed, and just as I wondered about the absence of other passengers the train pulled out. Dostoyevsky sat down on the lone bench and opened his book. He had just lowered his head when my mother came in from the street and I remembered that I had been brought here to be tried for the crime of waking the dead. I also knew that my mother was going to suggest that I plead guilty and apologize to the judge. *He's your father. My husband. I have my ways...* But I planned to stand on my own two feet and deliver an impassioned speech in my own defence. Throbbing with emotion and truth I would proclaim that the voices of the dead were the voices I needed to fashion the chaos of my own particular truth, that without them I was just a puny stick floating on—as I was seeking the appropriate body of water the dream lost its hold on me and I was just myself, at a bizarre tea party with my father, my mother, Dostoyevsky. They were so caught up in their own triangle they didn't even notice that I had drifted away and now returned. The cookies were gone. All that was left were a few bits of chocolate.

My father was leaning towards me. He looked angry. They must have been arguing again.

"You are the one who brought him into our lives. You are the one who insisted he live in our house. Not me, not your mother. Or have you forgotten that?"

"He felt sorry for him," my mother protested. "So did I. It was a kindness you should be proud of."

"Kindness! And was what you all did to me a kindness?"

My father was right. I did wake Dostoyevsky from the dead. I invited him into my dream, brought him into the present on my train, then rediscovered him in his alphabet-soup pyjamas, a shrivelled lunatic Moses carrying his twisted testament of good and evil down from the mountain of his insanity.

Dostoyevsky's eyes fastened to mine. At this moment I felt my feet sliding into his misshapen shoes, the rough cloth of his trousers scratching across my thighs, a cramping of the shoulders as his coat tightened across my back. Before I could stand to protest there was a crippling pain in my gut, the same place that tore with fear when Dostoyevsky, waving his pyjama bottoms defiantly, leapt from the ledge. The same place, I now know, Dostoyevsky was torn by his own panic as he fell towards the pavement.

As I struggled to my feet my father, too, was rising. Dostoyevsky looked on serenely. Now I was the one on the edge, about to take the leap. My fist was clenched and eager, swelling into a giant sledge ready to smash my father into what I would one day call the smoky light of memory.

My father, for the second time that afternoon, began a triumphant smile. As becomes so obvious when objectively recounted, as I should have known the whole time, my father had ensured he would be the one to script the final act. The pills he had taken were not for his heart. They were strychnine, rat poison; and the whole time we were drinking tea, eating cookies, trading insults, playing out the mock trial and each, in our own way, wondering what revenge he could find for the sins we had committed against him, he knew himself to be dying.

Even as my fist moved towards him and the voice I had finally woken was preparing to burst forth, my father must have been feeling his own final voice: blood filling his insides and rising to his throat as his organs exploded. He wavered behind his desk, deformed shoulder twitching, and parted his lips to complete his ghastly farewell, a rushing exodus of blood I can still see.

He slumped to the floor and I rushed to kneel over him. There were no last words, none of the comforts of forgiveness, and when I stood to call the police I found the others had left me. The door was open and the apartment suddenly more empty than the most deserted station. The man I had become washed his father's dishes, covered his father's body with a blanket, then walked out into the city. I would never see Dostoyevsky again. But when I got to the first corner my mother was waiting for me. Night had fallen and in the light of the streetlamps her dyed hair suggested the colours of autumn leaves. She slipped her arm through mine and we began to walk towards her apartment. When we reached the building she disengaged from me, closed her eyes and turned her cheek to be kissed.

A taxi had come into view. It was yellow, and the white light on its roof was glowing to indicate it was free. There was something of a misty light surrounding the taxi as it came towards us, and as though this was a dream I imagined it stopping for a moment while I climbed in, then speeding away while my mother continued to wait with her eyes still closed, her neck extended, her cheek offered.

But of course the taxi was unaware of my pretend dream. Though the mist was real, and the night's darkness like a cloak waiting to be slipped into. I put my hand on my mother's shoulder, bent towards her. Instead of slowing, the taxi accelerated. I could feel the soft comfortable weave of my mother's jacket beneath my palm. I pushed.

By the time the taxi's headlights picked up my mother's falling body, I was around the corner and covered by darkness. There was an unpleasant sound I couldn't avoid hearing. In the next day's paper there was an article about a man who committed suicide in the presence of his wife, so distressing her that within the hour she threw herself in front of a passing car.

For many years I carried the notice of the double funeral in my wallet. Until one night, after inflicting its story on a stranger, I burned it.

Shortly before his death in December 1999, Matt Cohen won the Governor General's Award for his novel *Elizabeth and After* and the Harbourfront Festival Prize in honour of his life as a writer. His previous novel, *Last Seen*, was a finalist for both the Governor General's Award and the Trillium Award, and was chosen by Margaret Atwood as Best Book of 1996 (*Maclean's*). In 1998 he received the Toronto Arts Award for Writing. He is the author of thirteen novels as well as poetry, collections of short stories, books for children and works of translation from French to English. Matt Cohen lived with his family in Toronto.